D1823393

The Mystery of Millions

A Novel

By Lloyd E. Scott

Time

Days

Weeks

Months

Years

Age

Older

Single

Alone,

The Present

THEN…A shock

A sudden change

The Mystery of Millions

Dramatis Personae

Alfred—The guy

Claire—The woman

Oscar—The accountant

Margaret—The neighbor

Ben---The big boss who owns the newspaper

Anna—The young journalist at Ben's Newspaper

Dr. Wong---The doctor in the dream

Betty---The older woman where Anna works

The Mystery of Millions

Winter. Seattle, Washington. Alfred is alone now. No longer married. Now he is alone and free. Finally. He decided to go to Seattle for a bit. He likes the cold and the fresh air. He is deciding where he wants to be currently in his life. He is getting older now and is almost seventy. For once he is happy. He lets his hair grow a bit due to the cold. But then after a week or two he knows that he must shave it. And that is what he does. The day went fast. It is a cold day. He got something to eat and now he has decided that he wants to go downstairs and explore the bar next door before it

gets crowded with the young crowd.

Alfred takes stock in the place as he sits down

and is waited on immediately by a young waitress in her

middle twenties. She flirts with him. He smiles in kind.

He looks at the posters on the wall of the players who

used to play for the local sports teams. As the waitress

returns he gives her a twenty-dollar bill. He takes a sip

of his strong drink. An older woman in her seventies

enters the bar. She looks around the room and sits at a

table that faces Alfred. He doesn't notice her at first.

Not until a few minutes later. The waitress takes the

lady's order and then she heads to Alfred's table and

gives him his change. He gives her five dollars. She

smiles as she pops her gum that she is chewing. The

older woman holds her head down. Alfred glances at her

and smiles in kind. She manages a smile. The waitress hands the lady her drink and she give the waitress a ten-dollar bill. After taking a sip, she glances at Alfred and motions him over to her table. He turns around to see who she is motioning to. But he knows that she is motioning to him. Nodding his head, he gathers his drink and sits at her table.

"Are you okay? You look sad," he asks.

"I'm fine," she says softly. "I was married for many years. But as in the case of many men, he got his hands caught where they should not have been caught. Thirty years down the damn drain. Makes no sense, huh?" she asks, sipping her drink.

"No. It does not. I'm sorry. Really sorry," he says apologetically.

"I know you are. You seem very sincere," she says, sizing him up. "You are new to the area. You don't look like a Seattle person."

"What do you mean?" he asks, giggling.

"Yeah right. You know. Right?"

"Yes I do. I've been here twice over the years. They're different. That's for sure," he says.

"I don't mean to pry. But what brings you here?"

"I like cold weather. I'm originally from the bay area. After I finally got out of my last marriage, I bolted. I want to move to Anchorage, Alaska. I can always watch my church and Sunday school on zoom thanks to the pandemic. Nothing has been the same since. That virus really did mess up things," he says, sipping his drink.

"You're out. Did you want another one?" she asks.

"I better not. I know it's not that strong but I'm okay for now."

"What happened with the marriage?" she asks.

"Lack of communication and outside people influencing the marriage. They should have minded their own business than get into ours. You know what I mean?"

"Yes I do. Our son was an addict. We thought that he would get his act together. But he never did. We got tired of giving him money for his habit and trying to get him clean. Then one day we got a knock on our door. Mr. and Mrs. Peters, your son is dead. We're very sorry. Do I think that had anything to do with the divorce? I do. He was our only child. This is what we get in return. I just don't understand it. It makes no sense. But we were having problems anyway before our son acted a fool. You never know how your children will turn out. You don't look as if you have any kids," she says.

"You're right. I don't. I did not want them at first. But then I changed my mind. My first wife was not having it. She was adamant that she was not going to have children under any circumstances. Sometimes I wish that I had one. Other times I am glad that I don't have any. So many homeless these days. Drug addicts. Alcoholics. Mentally ill who should be in a mental facility. Not to mention violence in the streets. It's a mess. It's a mess."

"I agree. It is indeed a mess. Yeah," she says, staring into her glass before taking a big gulp which causes her to frown. "You did not answer my question. Or maybe I did not ask. You're new here. You told me why. Where are you staying? Next door?" she wonders.

"Yes. Next door. Nice place. Nice hotel. Very clean and classy. I like it."

"You appear as a classy person, and I can tell that you are very educated. You probably have a graduate degree. Right? Believe me I can tell," she says, eyeing him.

"Yes. I have an MBA. Better late than never. I got it late in life. And I did it all online. The MBA was easy. Just a lot of writing. The undergrad was a chore with a few classes. I had to take over 40 classes. Only a few of my classes from many years ago that I took transferred. I was not thrilled about that. But onward I pushed and onward I went."

"I can tell that it is important to you. You speak of it with joy in your heart," she says. Clearing her throat, she blushes as she holds her head down. "You want to go back to your room. Geez. I know how that sounded but I thought that I would ask. I know. I know. You probably think that it's silly of me asking you to go to your room with me. Here I am an over seventy-plus woman with wrinkles on my face sitting in a bar having a drink. Alone. And now I am asking you to let's go to your room. Silly," she says, embarrassed.

He holds out his left hand and touches her right hand. He smiles that comforting smile of his. Getting to his feet he waits for her to stand as well. He smiles at the bartender and hands her five bucks. They head to the front door. Alfred holds the door open for the woman.

"You never told me your name."

"Oh. Silly me. Claire. My name is Claire. And you are?"

"Alfred. Really. That's my name," he says.

"I believe you. You might find it odd that I am in this bar. And here I am talking to a gorgeous black man. Huh?"

"Not at all. I am older than I look. Before you ask I'm seventy. My back lets me know of my age. It has been doing that for years now. Such is life," he says.

"Wait. Wait," she says, stopping. "You're seventy? Really? I know---black men don't show their age. Really?" she asks, looking him over.

"Yes ma'am. Really. Time flew by after I got my first divorce. Time flew by."

The hotel is right next door to the bar. He opens the door, and she follows him. He smiles as he passes by the front desk. The young woman smiles and waves

at him. They turn to the right and head to the elevator

which is open. He presses for the fifth floor and the

doors close. They glance at one another for a moment.

The elevator stops and the doors open. He exits first and

waits for her. They head to the right and walk to the

middle of the hallway. He stops and pulls out his card

key and presses it onto the door. The door opens and he

enters first. She follows and he closes the door and turns

on the lights. He closes the curtains and places the card

key into the drawer by his bedside. He reaches inside of

another drawer and pulls out a bottle of scotch. Heading

to the small fridge he opens it and pulls out two cans of

sodas.

        "Yes please," she says, as she takes the bottle

from him.

He gets two plastic cups. She pours some of the scotch into the cups. She takes a swig of the scotch before pouring the soda, into both of their cups.

"Are you okay?" he asks.

"I am," she says, softly.

"What are you looking for? I mean I know that you said your husband left you after many years. And I know that you're angry and hurt. But---."

Before he can finish his sentence she grabs his face, kisses him, and holds him tightly.

"You must think that I'm silly. I know," she says, holding him tightly and fighting back the tears. "Many years of being together. Then I find out that he's been cheating for a while. Damn it!" she says, sobbing.

He pats her on her back over and over. Eventually she contains herself.

"Listen. Lie down and relax. Nothing must

happen. You'll be okay."

Two Days Later

Alfred had not heard from the woman, Claire,

after that day. He did not think anything of it. He

figures that she needed time alone. He prays that she is

okay. After finishing breakfast ad sipping his coffee,

there is a knock on his door. He figures that it must be

her. Heading to the door and peering out of the

peephole, he cannot believe who it is. As he opens the

door, two police officers look at him.

"Yes?"

"Are you Mister Alfred?" the tall, older man

asks.

"Yes."

"May we come in?" he asks.

"Sure. Please," he says, opening the door and sitting on a chair facing the officers.

The officers enter the room and close the door. The tall police officer pulls out an envelope.

"You were with an older woman last night. Her name was Claire Peters."

"Oh. Yes. I was with her. Is everything okay?" Alfred asks.

"No. Everything is not all right. She overdosed yesterday."

"Oh my God," he sighs, holding his head down.

"Are you alright?"

"Oh my God. She was upset about her ex-husband. She cried in my arms. Oh my God."

The police officers look at one another. The tall one hands Alfred an envelope.

"This is for you. Read it. She left it near her body."

Alfred takes the envelope and opens it. There is a check enclosed face down. It reads:

'My dear Alfred. You are very sweet. I am sorry about all of this. But I cannot go on. Enjoy life because we do not know when our life will be over. Enjoy your wealth given to you from me. Claire."

He turns over the check. It is for five million dollars. He looks at the police officers.

"What is this about? Is this real?" he asks.

"Yes. You don't know who she was?" the officer asks.

"No."

"You've never heard of the Zeus family here in Seattle?"

"I'm a native Californian. I read a lot, but I never heard of the Zeus family. I take it they're rich," he says.

"Very rich. They own land here. Lots of land. Zeus is her maiden name. Now you're rich. And you're going to get richer. Take care, sir. Are you going to be okay?"

"Wow. I'll be okay. Goodness me. What the hell?" he says, still in shock.

"Have a good day sir," the other officer says, as the two men leave and close the door.

Alfred could not believe the news, the envelope, and certainly not the check. But everything is real. He is now a millionaire. He lies on his bed confused. A few moments later he decides to go downstairs and have

a drink at the bar. He takes his drink and sits in the

lounge. An older man who looks like an accountant,

dressed in a plaid suit with a bow tie and holding a

briefcase, approaches the young woman at the desk. She

tells the man that the man who he is inquiring about is

right over there on the chair. He heads over to the chair

and introduces himself. They shake hands.

"I know you heard about Miss Claire. I am

sorry. I can tell that you two must have had a good time

together. She was very nice but lonely after her husband

of many years cheated on her. Are you okay?" the man

named Oscar says.

"As well as can be expected. Good Lord. Five

million dollars for me."

He laughs from disbelief.

"My name is Oscar, by the way. You think that's something," he says, smiling showing his teeth. "Wait until I tell you something else. Take a deep breath. Okay. Here goes and I am not kidding. In case you do not know, she did not have any heirs. She and her husband settled their divorce without any drama. That is all over. Her only son died. There are no other heirs. She met you. She liked you. We met at my office yesterday. You are the sole owner now. Her home is fully paid for. We do not want outsiders to buy that mansion. We want to keep someone local to own it. You are searching where you want to be since your divorce. We want you to live in it. The home is fully furnished. While you are thinking about that," he says, he reaches inside of his briefcase and pulls out a check. He gives it to Alfred who in turn looks at the man with shock and disbelief on his face. "I know this will come as a shock to you, but it's yours. The Zeus family are filthy rich. Many died over the years. You own the estate now. Really."

Alfred blinks his eyes as he looks at the check once more. Still not believing what he sees, he looks at the accountant and shakes his head. He looks around the room nervously, and then at the accountant.

"Are you serious?" Alfred asks, whispering.

"Yes," he says, smiling. "It's yours. All yours. Twenty-five million dollars."

Alfred gulps down his drink. The accountant asks him if he wants another one. Alfred declines.

"I don't think so. Good Lord. What a day this has been so far. Where is her mansion that you speak of?" Alfred asks.

"Three blocks north of here then you turn right. You can't miss it. It's all white with big black doors. Let me take you there. You need to check out of the hotel first. Get your things."

Alfred does not believe anything that is going on. He still wonders whether all of this is true or not. It is. But he does not want to believe it.

2

"Are you feeling better?" Mr. Oscar asks, leaning over Alfred with a bottle of cold water in his hand.

"Huh? What?" he asks, looking around the room confused and in a daze.

"I said are you okay? Are you feeling better?" Mr. Oscar asks, again.

"I'm not sure. What. What happened?" he asks, slowly sitting upright on the couch.

Mr. Oscar laughs.

"As soon as you entered the house you looked at the massive ceilings and the long hallways. You looked at me and then, boom! There is where you fell. I caught you in time before you hit your head on the floor and I

dragged you to the couch. Are you feeling better now?"

"Wow! What a trip!" he says, opening the bottled

water and drinking the entire contents.

"I guess you were thirsty. Go on with your

questions," Oscar says.

"I'm sure her surname is not Zeus," he says,

laughing.

"And I'm sure that it does not matter whether she

is Polish or Jewish. It does not matter what her real

surname is so forget it. They lost money in the war

years ago. Many of her family were killed. She was the

last one who survived. She only had one child with her

husband. As you probably are aware, he was a drug

addict and he died. Poor thing. You know about her

husband. And don't worry about him. When they met

he had his own money already. He was and still is an

attorney. He won't bother you. She is the one who took

the divorce the hardest not him. Listen. There are

telephone numbers for everything. You have a chauffeur

at your disposal. The only weird thing is her room. As

you can imagine her closet is full of her stuff. You can

sell it if you want. I can imagine that must be weird for

you to live here and sleep in there, and her stuff is in the

closet."

"Oh uh. It's her stuff so whatever. If I don't see

any ghosts or hear weird noises I am sure that I will be

okay," Alfred says, managing a smile.

"Listen," Oscar says, checking his watch. "I

better go. Here is my card. If you need anything call me

anytime. Oh, and this place is soundproof. You can

play your music as loud as you want. If you want. Oh.

As for the ghosts that you mentioned---old houses have their own noises and souls."

"I know what you mean. I will be fine. I don't get spooked easily. I don't do play loud music anymore. I would play piano. I'm not sure if I told you or not but I am a pianist and I sing. That is what I will be doing. That is good to know that the place is soundproof. I will not disturb anyone," he says, smiling at the accountant.

"If you're ever up late and you look out of the window, don't be surprised if you see a light coming from across the street. The old bird who lives there is a widow and looks out of her window at night. Don't take it personal. I will let myself out. There is a stocked bar. Relax and make yourself a drink. You look as if you need one. Desperately," Oscar says, smiling widely

again as he exposes his teeth. Oscar opens the front door
and leaves.

Alfred looks down the long hallway and decides
to explore it. He locates the bar in one of the rooms. He
makes himself a drink. Indeed, the bar is fully stocked
including crystal glasses. He smiles as he locates a
bottle of champagne. He is relaxed now as he heads
down the hall. He notices another living area that is very
quaint. He looks around the room and smiles. He
cannot believe his eyes. Here he is in this marvelous
well-kept mansion. And it's his. How is this possible?
And why him? This cannot be real. Someone taps him
on his right shoulder, and he cannot believe it. Slowly,
he turns around. Claire is looking at him with a smile.
He shrieks.

"No. No. Please do not faint. You are not dreaming. I am a spirit now. But I did commit suicide which is not good."

"Indeed. Were you that upset?" he asks, trying to stay calm.

"Yes. You---came a bit too late. I thought perhaps that---" she says, as she stops and holds her head down. "I thought that maybe you and I---but you came just a bit too late. A day late in fact."

"I don't follow. You told me about your ex-husband and so did Oscar," he says.

"Oscar. Oh my. What a character he is," she says, laughing. "God bless him. He has kept my finances well. I mean. I don't splurge. I have more than enough money. But he does keep everything in order especially my assets. He might not have told you what I own. But I own a lot. And now it's yours. I see

your face. It is still confused. My dear man, don't be

confused. Think about it. How many times have people

said oh if I only had money I would do this and this?

Now it is your turn. You are a handsome man. I know

about the internet and dating. You have good sense. I

can tell. When the time comes when you are ready for,

you know. Companionship. Be careful with who you

date. You will probably meet somewhere for coffee.

But if you hit it off okay, then you will bring her here.

You don't own anyone an explanation when that time

comes, so don't say anything about where it came from.

You're an artist and you're going to succeed."

      "What do you mean?" he asks, as his eyebrows

rise.

"I've seen it. It will come out of nowhere. You will be known. They will want to interview you. You don't have to tell them anything about here."

"This mansion is very grand if I might say so. But. I'm still a bit confused," he says.

"Don't be. You won't be able to see me, but I am always here. I left my stuff in the closet. You see? I will always be here with you. You still don't get it. Do you? I'm sorry. I know this is hard for you. I'm sorry. But when I saw you, I saw a kind face and a kind person. I see the pain on your face. I understand. I've been there."

"Had you planned on---you know?" he asks.

"Yes. It has been in the planning stages for a long time. Believe it or not, had you not been in that bar that evening, when I got home I was going to do it. I

The Mystery of Millions

know you think that I am a silly old woman. I was

lonely and pissed off. Here I was divorced from a man

after all those years. It's not fun being a lonely woman

who is now divorced and over seventy. We all have

needs, sexual needs. I know I do. At the hotel you let

me cry my eyes out. And you held me as a caring

person. I wanted more and to maybe, sleep with you.

But I know that had I done that I probably would not

have gotten anything out of it other than sexual

satisfaction. Don't look sad. Please do not look sad. I

am where I am supposed to be. I was never a believer as

you are. Correct?" she asks.

"Yes. How. How did you know that?" he

wonders, frowning.

"It's on your face sweetie. Your face reveals a

lot about you. It's on your face. You are a kind person

who has made mistakes in your life. There is something missing in your life. It's called love. I'm sure you're divorced as you told me, but you were probably married before that too. But there's nothing like the first woman in your life. Am I right?"

"Yes," he says, softly, as he whispers and holds his head down.

Thunder is heard in the sky as it cracks. He turns and looks down the hall. Then. It begins to pour. He smiles because he loves the rain.

"Listen. Someone is headed this way. You better not be seen talking to me. Or I should say, talking to the air. Just remember that I am always with you and be careful. You are a private person. But you know there are some people who will come out of the woodwork and be nosy, like the person coming to your

day. She's a newspaper reporter. Be careful."

"Huh? What?" he asks.

His doorbell is rung. He heads to the door and

looks out of the curtain. It is pouring down rain. A

young woman in her late thirties with a dark raincoat and

umbrella is at the door. She has on a lot of make-up and

comes across as knowing how attractive she is with that

conceited smile. He opens the door and tells her to enter

the gate. She does so and closes the gate from behind

her, as she heads towards the door and enters. He closes

the door.

"It's a bit wet out there. And who might you

be?" he asks, being polite.

"I am Anna," she says, smiling holding out her

right hand to shake his hand.

He shakes her hand and takes the umbrella from her and places it into the umbrella stand.

"May I take your coat?"

"Now then," he says, heading to the restroom and laying her coat over the bathtub. "What brings you here on a night like this? Or need I ask?" he asks, approaching her.

She smiles. He notices her mini skirt that shows off her toned tanned legs.

"You are the new owner. Word got out. And here I am interviewing you."

"But I do not want to be interviewed. I have nothing to say. You know the story I am sure. I don't mean to be rude. But I don't want any news or interviews about me. I am sure that people know about her and how sadly, she committed suicide. And now here is this black guy living in her mansion that she

bequeathed to me. Oscar told me that she had no heirs

and that most of her people are Polish. They lost many

members of the family in the war. That is all that there

is to it. Sorry if I come on strong. I apologize," he says,

containing himself.

"I know how you feel. I'm sorry. I did not mean

to be so strong and come on strong either. It's just that

you know when the news hit we were all curious. Then

we found out that you know. You're---you. A black

guy. No offense to you but she was not one who came

across as dating someone out of her race. She was very

nice and easy to talk to if you were able to get into her

circle. But other than that, she was very private and a

lady. If you know what I mean. She was truly one of

the rare ladies that I have ever met in my lifetime. You know what I mean?" she asks, looking into his eyes.

"Yes. Yes. I know exactly what you mean. As for me being, you know, not like you or the others, white, it happens. Race should not play a key in anyone's life. But, sadly, it still does in many peoples' lives. I know what you mean though. It's okay. Please, let's get out of this room and head to the back room. You know I still have not explored the entire house yet. Oscar told me about the bedroom and how she left a lot of things. I will leave them as they are also," he says, as the head to the back of the house.

He enters the room and turns on the lights to another elegant room. A flat screen sits above the mantle. He notices the wet bar and smiles. The entire room is carpeted and there is a chandelier hanging in the center of the room. Two big wing chairs are opposite

one another. And a chaise lounge is on the left side

overlooking the garden. He smiles.

"Gorgeous," Anna says, smiling.

"Yes. It is. And another bar. Love it. What's

your pleasure?" he asks.

"Any champagne down there?"

"Oh. A woman to my own heart.""

"Huh?" she asks.

"Oh uh. Champagne is my guilty pleasure.

That's what I meant. Let's see," he says, bending down

and looking into the small refrigerator. He smiles when

he sees several expensive bottles of champagne. He

pulls one out and closes the fridge. "Voila!" he says,

smiling. He reaches for two glasses and holds the

champagne in the other hand. He opens the champagne and pops the cork.

Anna jumps nervously and smiles. He pours the champagne in both glasses, then places the bottle onto the table.

"Cheers," he says, making a toast.

They touch glasses and sit down.

"Yum. This is very good," she says.

"Glad you like it. I hope you ate something before you came over here. It's not very smart to drink on an empty stomach. I learned that from over the years. Believe me."

"Oh no. I'm fine. I had a big lunch. That was hours ago but I'm fine," she says.

"What's the real reason why you're here? I know what you do as a writer/journalist. But why are you here. Really?"

"I---I don't know what you mean exactly. What do you mean?" she asks, smiling as she sips her champagne.

"Yeah right. You've probably lived here for many years in Seattle and are used to the rain and cold. But you're here with me, a stranger during a storm wearing a mini skirt. And as they say, eyes are the reflection of the soul. I see your eyes and I see sadness. People say the same thing about me. And now I am saying that to you. It's okay. We all have a story and a past. What's your story?" he asks, sipping his champagne, as he crosses his legs and looks at her.

She smiles again, nervously. She is doing her best to be cool and act cool. But she knows that he is right in his assessment.

"Why am I here? You already know that. We know the story. We don't believe it, but we know that it's true. Everyone knows Oscar and he confirmed the story. I guess it makes sense because Claire does not have family. And even if there is some long lost relative in Poland somewhere, she left everything to you. Now don't you find that hard to believe considering that you just met her the other day in the bar?" she wonders.

Now he is put on the spot. Now it is his turn to answer while she checks out his body language.

"Sorry. What was your question?"

She giggles.

"I said don't you find it a bit odd that you two just met the other day in a bar and she left you all of this and money? I find that very strange," she says, honestly.

"I understand and I understand how many people feel about that. But you're young. When you're a senior citizen and you're by yourself, it's not any fun. Not really. I enjoy being by myself because of the peace and quiet. But there's nothing like having someone there with you. Not just for sex at our age but for having someone there with you. When she came into the bar I noticed her. I was sitting alone at a table and then she came in. Her sadness, loneliness and hurt were all over her face. It was obvious. When I looked at her and she noticed me, she got up and asked if it was okay if she could sit with me. I acquiesced and we started talking. She had one drink and then she said that she wanted to get out of there. She asked if I was staying at the hotel up the street and I told her yes. That's where we ended up. As soon as we got in there and I closed the door she kissed me passionately. I got it and I understood what was going on. We did not have sex. She looked pale and very sad, but I could still see her youth. I could tell that she looked good from years ago. After she told me about her ex-husband, then I got it and I understood. Poor little thing. She talked her guts out to me and she cried. I held her and I let her cry on my shoulders. You know she was hurt a lot. I know that he cheated on her, but it must have been more than that and very deeply."

"May I have more please? I'm out," she says, handing him her glass.

He reaches for the glass and refills it. She smiles warmly.

"You should smile more. You have a nice smile."

"Thanks," she says, sipping her champagne and looking around the lavish room. "Okay. She took it hard because his secretary who he left her for, she has been over here a few times during holiday season. They threw good parties, and his secretary was here. She never knew about the two of them until he started working late. His habits changed. That is always a red flag. When she found out that he had been with her she was crushed because she had been in their house a few times before. She did not cry, and they had an amicable divorce. But she was hurt. Poor little thing."

"Indeed. I can tell that you liked her," he says.

"I did. He wasn't worth it. Now he's happy because he's getting some young pussy! Men!

Sometimes you guys make me so mad. Sometimes!" she says, angrily, sipping her champagne. "I'm sorry. You seem like a nice guy."

"I didn't mean to strike a nerve. But it looks as if I did. Who was the lucky guy who broke your heart?" he wonders, looking into her watery eyes.

"Yeah right. My fucking boss. Sorry for swearing. I was working on a thorough peace one night some time ago. Not many people work at night. I was bending over at the filing cabinet. He came in and grabbed me by my rear end. I almost hurt my finger because I was flipping through the files. I looked at him with disdain on my face. He told me to come into his office. He closed the door. Damn asshole," she says, holding her head down and sobbing.

"But. Did he do anything?"

"He grabbed my hand and put it on his dick. I was pissed and I ran to the door. He told me that if I ever told anyone about that he would fire me. I'm sure when I saw his wife at parties that they gave at their house, she must have known something by the expression on my face," she says, gulping her champagne.

"I'm sorry. Truly. Is that why you're here? I'm a good listener."

She glances around the room nervously. He can tell that she is uncomfortable, but he has no idea why. She sighs and is about to say something when lightning lights the sky. They both glance at the window. He gets off his chair and heads to the window to close the curtains. As it becomes dark he turns on the lights.

"Are you okay?" he asks.

"Yeah. I am," she says, looking at him with her sad eyes. Her face is still red from getting upset with what she just shared with him about her boss.

He frowns as he shows that he cares, and he feels her pain. She glances at him, and he wipes her face. Taking a gulp of champagne from her glass, she smiles and shows him once again that the glass is empty.

"I'm sorry. Very sorry. You asked why I was here. Now you know why. I don't like being alone. But I know that most men just want sex. Look at me and I am sure that you see why," she says.

"You are a beautiful woman and you do have nice legs. Would you like an aspirin to calm your nerves?" he asks.

"Yes. And more champagne if that's okay with you," she says, smiling.

"Of course, it is. I guess the lady of the house and myself had one thing in common: champagne. There are quite a few bottles in there," he says, getting off his chair and heading to the bar.

"Yes. Yes. There was a lot of champagne flowing at their parties. Dom Perignon of course. Only the best," she says, getting comfortable on the couch. "I love this place. You are so lucky to be in it."

"Thanks," he says, coming from behind the bar with a bottle of champagne that he opened. "But. Why are you here?" he asks, pouring the champagne into her glass and handing it to her.

"Thanks," she says, taking the glass from him.

"Are you okay? You've been slamming down the glasses. Did you want something to eat?"

"We can order pizza. No problem," she says, as she opens her phone and pushes a button and orders a pizza. They have her debit card information, and she gave them the address. They're on the way. It's good pizza," she says, smiling, as she closes her phone. "Yes. Yes. I know. You asked me a question."

"Yes. I did. What's the answer?" he asks, as he presses the issue.

"Yeah right. You know the answer. I told you one of my issues. It's always there. I have this body and that is what everyone looks at. I have more education than most where I work. They're not impressed with that. All that they look at is my body. Especially my legs. Yes. It pisses me off. Sorry for coming on strong but it makes me angry. You seem like a cool person to talk to and that is why I am telling you this. I'm sure you know that I am here to find out more about you. To find out who you are and why she gave you the money and the house. Did I answer your question?"

"Yes. You did. Sorry if I struck a nerve."

He turns on the television to change the subject and for background noise. He looks at this young attractive woman. She is right. She is gorgeous even without the heavy make-up and jet-black hair that she dyes in certain places. The doorbell is rung. He gets off the chair and looks out of the curtain. He opens the door and hands the delivery guy a twenty-dollar bill and tells him to keep the change. Closing the door and locking it, he heads to the kitchen and reaches for a big plate and napkins. He heads to the back room where she is and stops in his tracks as he notices that she is out like a light and spilled her drink.

3

About an hour later she comes to and looks around the room. She is embarrassed. Her hair is all over the place. She composes herself and sits upright on the chair.

"Oh dear. What happened?" she asks, embarrassed, as she looks at him.

"You were out like a light. I let you be. I did not want you to think that I did anything to you. Or tried to get fresh with you. I told you to eat something. There's the pizza. Help yourself. I don't think that you need anything else to drink. Did you want some coffee?" he asks, politely.

"Yes. Please," she says, as she reaches for a slice of pizza and a napkin.

She is embarrassed. She does not know what to say as she eats and tries to compose herself. He gets the coffee ingredients and presses the button on the coffee maker.

'I don't know why Claire did what she did either," he says, sitting on his chair. "I was in the bar before her. She came in and sat down and her table was facing my table. We saw each other and made eye contact. She got out of her chair over. She sat opposite me, and we chatted. After one drink she said that she wanted to get out of there. My hotel is next to the bar and that's where we went. We talked. Nothing else happened. She left after a short period of time. I had not seen her nor spoken to her in a couple of days. Then one morning, I got a knock on the door of my hotel room. It was the police who told me what happened. When I was informed that she left me money, lots of money, I was floored and confused. If there were any surviving relatives she had no contact with them. I met the accountant when he showed up at my hotel room. And he told me what was going on. I figured that everything was real. He gave me a check. I looked at it and we went to my bank to deposit it. Now you know the whole story. I know. It makes no sense but that's the whole story. Now and then I can hear her voice which is odd. Then you came along today. Odd," he says.

"Oh my. I see. Because of what you just told me, when I tell you something, maybe you won't be too scared," she says, wiping her face with her napkin.

"What do you mean?"

"Hmm. This place is haunted," she says.

"What do you mean? She hasn't been dead that long. What do you mean this place is haunted?"

"It's haunted. This place was here when she bought it. She did upgrades to the house, obviously. But we always heard that this place is haunted. It has always been haunted so we were told. That is the story that everyone was told about this house. What people do in their homes is their privacy. There was a rumor that it is haunted because of people who died here over the years. Now then. You said that now and then you hear her, and she speaks to you. You don't find that odd?" she asks, taking a bite of her pizza.

"My mom told me years ago that she is psychic sometimes. I think that I got some of her abilities. I guess maybe when I first moved in she spoke to me to keep me safe. I don't know."

She laughs.

"You don't really believe that. Do you?" she asks.

"I don't know what to believe. I believe in haunted houses and mean people, demons, and that sort. If you say that is what you heard about this place then whatever. But you never answered my question. I did not forget."

"Yes. I know. You're right. I am here to find out about you per my editor. My boss. You know that. I am here now and you're interesting. I will tell him that. But you are more than interesting. And I see why she left you money and this gorgeous mansion," she says, gazing at the very high ceiling. "Gorgeous. Simply gorgeous. You know this is just the beginning."

"I know. But unlike others who will pry and knock on the door or ring the doorbell, when I see them I will ignore them. You were a different case. I figured out who you were, and I was right. But I decided to let you inside because you looked nice. And yes because you're beautiful. Let's face it. The Lord does not make everyone gorgeous or give them nice legs like yours. Get over it. It's a blessing from Him. Are you going to answer my question?" he presses.

"I thought that I had. I am here to find out about you. And to find out why you. Why did this rich lonely old lady who never met you before leave you all that money? It just does not make any sense. Sorry. You say that you two met in the bar. You noticed each other and you noticed her sad face and eyes. You went back

to your hotel room where she talked to you deeply about

her life. And vice-versa. Two days passed by with no

communication from her. There is a knock on your

door, and it is the cops. They tell you what happened

and then here comes Oscar. He tells you that the old

lady left you money and the mansion. Right? Is that

about it?" she asks.

"That's it. You hit the nail on the head," he says,

sipping his champagne.

She laughs.

"You know the funny thing is I believe you. But

it is weird and even you must admit that. Right?

Right?" she asks, looking at his eyes.

"Yes. But it's true. Every word of it. Sorry that many people will not believe it. But it's all true. Every word of it."

He glances at the curtains and heads over to open them and look at the clouds. It has stopped raining, but it is dark now.

"I see. I can't figure any of this out. And you know when I tell this to my boss he won't believe a word of it," she says, adamantly.

"I know," he says, turning around and facing her. "But eventually he will because it's true. Every word of it. And you know it is. Listen. I don't want this to sound bad. If you need a little cash I will give you some. I'm not implying that you need money, or that you are here to try to get some out of me. I was just thinking that if you know. If you needed some money I could throw you out a little cash," he says.

"I bet you could. I'm okay. I make do. I don't overextend myself though rents are high. I've taken more than enough of your time. I guess I better get going. You're a classy guy. You know that if there were other guys in your position, and I was at their place---well. You know," she says, smiling.

"Yes. I know. I'm not that kind of guy. I've never been like that. Many people think that I'm soft but I'm not. I've never been one of those rough and tough guys. That has never been my nature."

She gets off the chair and heads towards him. He gets off his chair and stands. She gets close to him. She sizes him up as she controls herself. She smiles as she caresses his face.

"You're very special. Can I come over again? Would that be okay?" she asks, hesitantly.

"Sure. Why not?"

They stare at one another before heading to the front door. He unlocks the door and shakes her hand. She leaves. He closes the door and locks it and looks at her as she heads to her car. She gets into her car and drives off. She only drives a few blocks before she stops the car and turns off the ignition. She pulls out her cellphone.

"Oh. It's you," her boss says.

"Yes. I'm just leaving now."

"And?"

"Nothing. He's on the level though the story is weird. But it's true."

"How do you know it is true, Anna? Does any of this make any kind of sense to you?" he asks, angrily.

"It does not. I had too much champagne to drink. I passed out for over an hour. He was a gentleman."

"Meaning what? He did not molest you?" he asks, giggling.

"Exactly, boss. Unlike you and other men he did not molest me. He was kind the whole night. He was honest. He admired my legs, but he did not make a pass at me. I know that it is a crazy story, and it does not make sense. But it's real and honest. He is an honest man. It is on his face and his eyes. He has very kind eyes. You saw the picture in the papers."

"Yeah, yeah," he mumbles. "Where are you? Oh. You're just leaving his place. You can come on over if you want," he says, laughing.

"Yeah right."

"Hey. I gave you a raise didn't I? I used your hand to touch my dick. That's all I did. I did not force you into doing anything else. Did I?" he asks, angrily.

"You didn't," she says, sighing and embarrassed.

"Okay then. Did you tell him about me? Of course, you did. I hear it in your voice. Silly woman," he says, getting irritated.

"I was pissed and angry. He said that he could tell that something was wrong. I told him and all my anger came out. Don't get so excited," she says, trying to remain calm.

"Yeah. Yeah. Like I said. I'm here by myself."

"Yeah I heard you the first time. Damn," she says, glancing at the rain that has fallen.

"Well. Get moving," he says, as he hangs up the phone.

She hangs up her phone and puts it into her purse. She sits motionless for a moment before she starts her car. Driving towards her boss' penthouse apartment, she knows that she is an idiot and a fool. But she is on her way to his apartment.

"Why? Why do I do this shit? I am better than this. I am on my way over there. He is not interested in any other woman at work but me. Me. I guess because I'm young, petite with nice legs and a nice face. I guess he doesn't want to go after the young ones in the office. And just think. Just think. I could get that dirty bastard fired. But if I did he would do something drastic. And he might end my career. We can't have any of that," she says, to herself, aloud, angrily.

It begins to become windy. She drives cautiously now. The rain has stopped. A car slammed on its brakes in the other direction. Thank goodness no one was hurt or injured. The person came to a yellow light and decided to slam on the brakes, rather than hit the accelerator. Very dangerous to do that but no one was hurt thank goodness. As she gets closer to her boss' place she drives slowly. Turning down a dark road, she stops and then she turns down a long road onto the high-rise expensive condos. She pulls up alongside the gate. She presses the button to let down her car window. The guard smiles because he recognizes her. She has been there before. The gate is opened, and she pulls her car into the gate and drives to the parking lot. Stopping her car and putting it into park, she turns off the ignition. Glancing at the top of the building, she can envision her

boss looking down from his window at the parking lot.
She is correct. He smiles and laughs heartily. She gets
out of the car and locks it and heads to the front door of
the building. Heading to the elevator she presses the
button. It comes immediately and she steps inside. She
presses 'P' for the penthouse. The doors close and she is
whisked to his floor. She looks at herself in the mirrored
glass of the elevator. Her face is sad and embarrassed.
She holds her head down and closes her eyes. The bell
chimes as the elevator reaches the penthouse floor. It
stops and the doors open. She exits from the elevator
and wipes her face. She heads down the hall and stops at
his door. Pressing the button, she hears him giggling.
He opens the door and sizes her up. She enters the
penthouse, and he closes the door.

"Don't worry, lover. I've had more than enough
to drink. I assure you I cannot get it up when I drink,"
he says, laughing.

She heads to the living room and sits on the
couch. He smiles as he closes the door. Heading over to
the chair opposite the couch, he stumbles and smiles.

"I guess I better make some coffee. Huh?"

"I'll do it," she says, heading to the kitchen.

She's been to his place several times. She knows
where things are. And she knows her way around the
kitchen.

"What uh. What did you find out?" he asks.

"He is a good guy."

"Huh? What you say?" he asks.

"I said that he is a good guy. He means well and
he is telling the truth. What he said happened and how

they met, is the truth. He's a good guy. He's telling the truth,"

"I'm not following you. What do you mean?"

She laughs.

"Everyone wants to know about him and how they met. I told you he is a good guy, and he told the truth. They met in a bar. He said that they both noticed each other as she walked into the bar. She sat down at his table, and they struck up a conversation. After they finished their drink they went up to his room at the hotel that is nearby. He said that all that they did was talk. She let out her emotions and cried on his shoulder. He said that she balled her eyes out. Whatever was troubling her she let it out with him. They were up late, and then she went home. He had not spoken to her in a few days and then the police knocked on his door and told him the news. How they knew about him one

wonders. Some kind of way they tracked him down.

Then our sweet little CPA got hold of him and met him.

He told him the news about the money that was left to

him. He was in denial at first, but then he realized that it

was true. They went to the bank and deposited the

money. He bid Alfred (yes, that's his name), adieu.

And Oscar left."

"Then eventually later you came to the door and

you two talked. Did you, uh," he says, looking at her in

a sexual manner.

"I flirted with him. Yes. He said that I have nice

legs and I am gorgeous. But he was not interested in me.

He said that he has an old saying: let the other dirty old

men go after the young girls. But he does look intently.

We drank champagne. I had too much to drink although

I had eaten something earlier. I started laughing a lot. He ordered pizza. I passed out. I woke up over an hour later and we ate. He said that I passed out, but nothing happened because he is a gentleman. I can tell that by looking at him. He is highly educated. Well-spoken. Dresses very well. And whatever cologne, oil, or after shave that he had on, he sure did smell nice. Goodness," she says, blushing, as she sits on the couch.

"Did you get a picture?"

"No. There was no need. I'm sure that his picture was taken when he went to the bank. And I'm sure that Oscar probably took a photo or something knowing him. And you, boss? How about you?" she asks, as she presses the issue and wants to know what he has to say about Alfred.

"I checked him out. He was arrested years ago in a domestic spat but nothing else. There's nothing else that I could find about him. I hate to say it, but you might be right. He seems as if he is okay and is just a guy. I thought for sure that we could find some dirt on him. After all, doesn't everyone have some dirt on them? We all did something bad in our past."

She shakes her head. She cannot believe what he just said. But considering that it is him, why should she be surprised? She knows how he is.

"Not everyone is like you or other men. I'm sure that you know what I mean. Oh," she says, glancing at the coffee pot that buzzed. "The coffee is ready." She heads to the kitchen to make coffee for them. She senses that he is looking at her in a sexual way.

"Cream and sugar or do you like it black as you do some of your women?" she asks.

"What?" he asks, giggling. "You're funny."

She brings the mugs over and places them onto the table. He takes his mug and sips it.

"Thanks. I like it nice and hot. Thanks. You're good. Very good. So," he says, placing the mug onto the table and leaning back on his chair. "Did you tell him about me? Or I should ask what you told him about me?" he asks, looking at her with a serious expression on his face.

She has seen this expression on his face before and she does not like it. Usually this means that he is about to go into a rage. But since he has been drinking a bit before she got there, she is not worried much.

"I did. They say that when you drink a bit you have loose lips."

"You do but only when you're licking. No. My dear. You are blunt and to the point. I have seen you when you're mad. You speak your mind. I like that. It turns me on. Well? Did you tell him about us?" he asks, again, looking forward to her answer.

"Yes. I did," she says to the point.

"I see. I never hurt you and I never penetrated you. Did I?"

"You did not. But you made me jack you off. That was gross," she says.

"I did not make you put it into your mouth. And I did not make you do anything that you did not want to do. I did not force you. Did I?" he asks, getting defensive.

"Yeah. I know. You did not."

"And you got a nice raise. I kept my word. Word got out about that raise and that's why people look at you mean. They're jealous," he says, sipping his coffee.

"How many were there?"

"Oh my. Look at you," he says. "You're getting feisty, aren't you? There weren't many. And many of them in the office don't look like you. They have mommies and daddies who have connections. That's how they got there where they are. I sure wish they could write like you. Have you ever paid attention to their writing, especially on the internet? Bleah," he says, embarrassed. "It's atrocious. They should be embarrassed by what they write. Yuck. You, on the other hand write quite well. Unlike those other college graduates, your writing shows and shines well. You're very smart. Not only do you have looks. You have brains."

"Thanks," she says, sipping her coffee.

"I see your expression. I really gross you out don't I?"

"Need you ask?" she asks.

"Do not forget that I am your employer."

"I can never forget that. What makes you happy? What makes you happy? I'm being serious here," she presses, as she looks at his pathetic, fat, sad face.

He gets off his chair and reaches for the brandy and pours a glass. He heads back to his chair.

"That is not going to help. I'm sure you know that. That's only a temporary solution to a longer problem. I'm being serious here. What makes you happy? There must be something that makes you happy. Right?" she says, as she continues to press the issue.

"I was young. Once. I met girls. I screwed lots of girls and women. I was married years ago. I have a daughter. Somewhere. I love young girls and women. My---wife got tired of that and she left me one day. She has been true to her word and never let me see my daughter. She is grown now. But I guess her mother must have poisoned her thoughts about me. And here I am, a successful man with lots of money. But also, a lonely man who screws beautiful women. They let me screw them because I have money. There is an old saying that says everyone has their price. You understand?"

"Yes. I do," she says.

She has never seen him like this. Being open about his life or previous life. But he has always been this way, chasing after skirts. He is now in his fifties and still doing the same thing. Chasing after skirts of young girls and women.

"And you? What about you? Since you opened that door. What makes you happy?" he asks.

"No kids for me if you're worrying about that. I am not a mother to be. And I don't ever want to be a mother. I never have. I am educated but I also have this body. I know that's what men look at. First, they look at my face and then at my body. Unlike many women, when I take off my make up I look like myself. I don't look like a normal bare faced woman."

"I know. I remember the first day that I saw you when you came into my office. I got a hard on like it was nobody's business. You are fine. Girl," he says, smiling widely, showing his yellow teeth from drinking coffee over the years, and not having his teeth cleaned regularly.

"Thanks. I guess. Are you happy with how you are? I'm being serious here."

"I---I---I don't want to talk about that. I am who I am. I am older now, and fatter. I drink too much sometimes, and I'm divorced. I have a kid and I miss her. But I made my bed as they say. And that is how it goes. You have a head on your shoulder. But you need to decide what you want out of life. By listening to you talk about him, Alfred, I know that something is there. Did you want to talk about it or not?" he asks, looking at her in her eyes.

"There is nothing to talk about. I told you that already. I am not a wife. I like my independence. Sure. Okay. I uh. I love sex and I like to be with someone. But I don't think that I could be with anyone for any length of time. You know what I mean? And to be with someone in the same house every day, sleeping with the same person every day in the same bed, that is not for me. I am not cut out for that."

"I understand that. But. You're still young. And you have a lot going for you. Really," he says, being serious for a change.

She does not say anything. She sips her coffee and stares.

"He---said that he has spoken to her," she mumbles.

"Oh? What's that? Oh. Does he know anything else about the house?"

"No. He doesn't. He does not."

"And you are going to see him again. Aren't you?" he asks.

She takes another sip of her coffee and places the mug onto the table.

"Yes. I must. It is what I do. It's okay. I will let my own self out."

He gets off the chair and heads to the door. As she stops, he also stops. Slowly, she reaches for the doorknob to turn it.

"Please. Listen. I know that I've had one too many but, uh. You know."

"You look and sound pathetic. It won't do you any good," she says, as she reaches for his zipper and unzips his pants. She reaches inside of his pants. She is

correct. Nothing happens as she touches his manhood.

"You see, this is what happens when you drink too much

or use too many drugs. You can't get it up.

As she opens the door and leaves. He stands in

the hallway with his pants down, as he looks at her walk

away.

4

       The storm subsided. It was calm for a bit. But then the wind picked up. Cars were heard screeching on the streets. Fire engines were heard roaring in the distance and then they got closer and closer. Dogs began to bark from the noise. Police cars decided to join the party. Clamor was everywhere for a bit of time. But then as soon as it had begun. It stopped. And it began to become quiet again. That lasted for a while. But that did not last long because the rain came en masse. It poured down. It lasted for a while. The wind caused the windows to rattle in the mansion. Alfred remained sleep through it all. For the most part. But then a sound began

to occur. It was the sound of a telephone.

He is in a deep sleep from the champagne that he

had with Anne. Suddenly, a telephone rings and rings

and rings again. He awakens and wonders where that

noise is coming from. Looking around the room he still

wonders where that noise is coming from. There it is

again. What in the world is that noise? Getting to his

feet he heads down the hall and turns on the light switch.

He hears the noise. No. Can it be? Is that really the

sound of a telephone? Where is it coming from he

wonders. Continuing to walk down the hall he hears it

ring again from behind a door. Hesitantly, he opens the

door and his fingers fumble along the wall. Finally, he

finds a light switch and turns it on. The room is

decorated Victorian style. He stands there from awe. As

the phone rings again, he finally locates it and heads

towards it.

"Yes? Yeah? Hello?" he asks, in a daze sitting

on a chair and yawning.

"Yes. Hello. Wake up. I am your neighbor

across the street. Wake up," an older woman says with a

strong voice. "Are you there?"

"Yes. It is after three in the morning," he says,

glancing at the clock on the wall.

"Yes. It is. I am a morning person and I go to

bed early, like 8 pm and sometimes earlier. That is why

I am awake."

"And who are you?" he asks.

"I told you. I live across the street. It is about

time that we meet and talk," she says, blowing smoke

from her cigarette.

"It's after three in the morning," he says,
groggily.

"Great. You can tell time. I'm a night owl. A
serious night owl. I'm downstairs in the main room. I'll
open the door and wait for you," she says, hanging up
the phone.

"Wait. Hello? I don't believe this. Has the
entire city of Seattle gone crazy with these women? My
goodness. What the hell," he says, as he hangs up the
phone.

He heads to the bedroom and puts on some
clothes and his boots. He brushes his teeth then he
shakes his head. Lightning causes him to jump for a
moment. But it is not raining now. Reaching for his
keys he opens the closet door and pulls out a long coat.

"This is nuts. This is nuts!" he says, aloud to himself.

Heading to the front door he turns on the lights and looks around the room. Opening the door, he steps outside. He closes the door and locks it. He shakes his head as he looks at the street, then he runs to the big house across the street. He rings the doorbell.

"I told you the door is open," she says, from inside her mansion.

He opens the door and closes it. She is standing in the middle of the room looking at him with a sheer nightgown on. She is of average height. She keeps her hair dyed black but that makes her look older. And she had a face lift.

"You can lock the door please. Now then. I am not like little miss tease who came to see you earlier today. I am bold and to the point and a bit aggressive.

But I'm to the point. Oh. I already said that. You keep

looking at me. Do tell. You think I look good for an old

broad or what?"

"Yes. I do. Of course, you've had plastic

surgery, but they did a good job. And you did not go

overboard and continue with plastic surgery. Good for

you. What's this all about or should I ask?" he asks,

honestly and confused, as he frowns.

"Like the others I am curious about this whole

thing with you, the deceased rich woman, and the

mansion. But I won't dwell on it as the others. You said

what happened and how you two met. I believe you.

I'm here to tell you to be careful. All eyes are on you.

You get it?" she asks, puffing on her cigarette and

putting it out in an ashtray.

He looks around the plush decorated room and looks to sit down.

"I need to sit."

"No. No. Please," she says, holding out her right hand. "Come upstairs with me. Please."

He looks at her face and hesitantly, gets off the chair and takes her hand. They walk up the plush staircase. She pushes a button on the wall and the lights are turned off below. He follows her down the very long hallway that has a plethora of doors just as his mansion also. She stops and enters her big bedroom with paintings adorned on the walls. He looks at the room with awe on his face. Locating a chair at the foot of the bed he sits and crosses his legs.

"You really are a gentleman. I can see why she fell for you. My. My," she says, smiling.

"Please don't say that. She did not fall for me. I am sure that you heard the story. But let me tell you how it really was without any embellishments. I was in the bar near the hotel. She came in a few minutes later. She looked around and I noticed her. She noticed me as well. Approaching my table, she asked if she could sit down. I said yes. She told the bartender she wanted a scotch and soda. The same drink that I was nursing. We talked and smiled. But as I was listening to her and looking at her eyes and face, I could tell that something was amiss. I was correct because soon after we finished our cocktails, she said that she would like to go to my room. We both blushed of course. Once we got there and she sat on the bed we talked and talked. I held her in my arms as she spilled her guts. She spent the night, but nothing happened, and she left the next morning.

"I went on about my business, but I was worried because I had not heard a word from her. I figured that she must have been busy or something. Two days later, while I was in my hotel room there was a knock on the door. By the intense knocking on the door, I figured it was a man. As I opened the door, two cops were standing at the door. They were very tall and looked menacing. They asked me if I knew this lady in the picture that they had. I told them yes. She and I had been together the other night. They both look at one another and tell me that she was found dead in her mansion. I held my head down and I was stunned. I told them that I was okay, and if they needed to ask me anymore questions they can. They left. Sometime later a knock was heard on my door, and it was the accountant. Oscar, I believe is his name."

"Oh my," she says, smiling. "Sweet, little Oscar. He is quite the character. I know that you probably could care less about him, but he is gay. Oh sure, he might have a wife, but he is gay. But whatever. What did he tell you? He told you about the money and your reaction was?"

"Yeah right," he says, yawning, and giggling. "When he told me that I looked at him and went blank. But looking at his face I could tell that he was serious. Then like you guys asking me questions, it was my turn to ask him questions. He was serious but I still did not believe him until we went to the bank. Then he took me to the house. I just stood there in total disbelief. Only when we went to the bank and deposited five million dollars in my account, did I believe him. But---this is still unbelievable. I'm still waiting for someone to wake me up."

She stares at him and sizes him up. She smiles widely before finally speaking.

"You really are a catch. Please," she says, holding out her right hand. "Sit with me."

"Uh. Listen," he says, embarrassed, as he blushes. "Once again it is late or early morning, depending on how you look at it. And I'm not feeling this right now. I don't know you or know anything about you."

"Knock it off will you? Please just knock it off," she says, in a serious tone. "Every woman in this town is going to try to get with you. Okay? You're not stupid. You are an educated man. All one must do is look at you. I know of the time, but you still speak the king's English. It is obvious. You are very different

than most Black men. You're different and I am sure

that you have heard that many times in your life. You

are very different. Listen," she says, sitting upright on

her bed and leaning against the headboard. "This whole

story is unbelievable. I agree. It's like when someone

wins the lotto, and you can't believe it. That is the way

this situation is. You won the lotto. Now here is

something that I wonder about. If it wasn't you and it

was someone else, would this same situation turn out as

it did for you? One never knows. I'm sure you know

that she had a son that died. Her husband died also. She

never remarried. And if there are any distant cousins

anywhere no one knows anything about them. And

don't worry. In case someone out of the blue does show

up claiming to be related to her, they will be laughed out
of the court."

"Okay," he says. "And what about you? What's
your take in all of this? Or are you just curious like the
others?"

"What you just said. I knew that people would
be coming in and out of there. Now it is my turn to see
you and to talk to you. Sorry I woke you up. I don't
want anything from you. No. that's not true," she says,
blushing, as she looks at his pants. "Listen. Sit right
there on that chair. There are many secrets that we all
have. Some secrets are best not known about. Some
people also have skeletons. Be careful while in that
house. There are secrets there and please don't ask.
Yes. Others will continue to show up unexpectedly, but
can you blame them? We have never seen you before.

And like I said, you do stand out. Just be careful and do what you're doing now. Don't say too much. You told me how you two met, and I believe you. It sounds like something out of a novel. I must admit that."

He yawns again as he tries to keep his eyes opened. She lies flat on the bed. As she is about to take off her nightgown he gets off the chair.

"Really. I must go. I can't stop yawning. Seriously."

"Is it because I am embarrassing myself?" she asks, embarrassed. "I know I must look like a silly old woman to you. I am rich. I live here by myself in this big mansion. And here I am throwing myself at you while wearing this sheer nightgown. Well," she says, as she looks at her nude body. "I did have on a nightgown," she says, getting in the bed.

"What are you afraid of? I see sadness on your face. What is it?" he asks.

Now it is her turn to feel uncomfortable as he looks at her with a serious expression.

"It's been a while since I've been with someone. I've lived here alone for many years. I know that I could make changes in my life. But I know that most men, especially young men, only want to be with me because of my money. And I feel like a fool sleeping with a younger man. I'm talking about any man fifty and younger. I'm seventy-four by the way. How old are you?" she asks.

"I just turned seventy believe it or not."

"Whoa!" she lets out loudly. "You sure don't look it that's for sure."

"No offense. But I am sure that you were a knockout when you were younger. And you kept yourself well. Money can do that. You have beautiful blue eyes and nice legs."

"Does it bother you that they're wrinkled?"

"I never thought about it. I am just here talking to you, looking at you and listening to you. I am not passing judgment because I'm here listening to you. That's all that I am doing. You mentioned something about secrets and the house. What are you talking about?"

Before she can answer the lights flash from the lightning that occurred.

"Oh my. Lightning. Thunder can't be too far behind. Wait for it," she says. "There it is. God or someone must be talking. I love thunder and lightning.

Do you?" she asks, smiling.

"Yes. As a matter of fact, I do love thunder and

lightning. And I love cool weather although my body

has issues with it as I have gotten older primarily my

lower back. It's nice to meet someone who likes cold

wet weather like me, and thunder and lightning too.

Nature is great. God is great!"

"Yes he is."

"Oh. Are you a believer?" he wonders.

"I am. But I don't go to church. I know I

should. Are you a believer? Need I ask? Silly me," she

says. "Of course, you are. Listen. Please. Listen.

Please," she says, in a comforting tone. "I get it and I

understand. But this is very real. Your life has changed

for the better. So far you are handling it well. Kudos to

you. I'm sorry but you're right. People will keep

bothering you to see if this is real and if the way it

happened with you two, really did happen that way.

They're jealous. That goes without saying. Of course.

Like you, many people have worked for a living. Some

people have been playing lotto for years and maybe have

won only a few bucks. I bet you never played lotto in

your life except maybe when it got high."

"Exactly."

"I figured as much," she says. "And here you are

now. Rich. Very rich. You did not win from playing

lotto. The Lord blessed you with that woman. You two

met in the bar. And the rest is history. Yes, I feel like a

fool for waking you up and asking you to come over

here. I don't know you and I never met you until now. I

am in my seventies with a new face and body. You can't

do anything about the aged spots though. And here I am trying to seduce you. I know. It makes no sense," she says, embarrassed, as she holds her head down.

He continues to look at her without saying a word. Everything that she said was right and dead on. She does look ridiculous with her sheer nightgown on and trying to seduce him. He sighs and shakes his head.

"You're right. My life has changed and none of this makes any kind of sense in the least. None of it. You're right, I don't believe any of this. Here's what I am going to do. I am going to close my eyes and wish all of this away because I know that this is not real. I know that this is not real because I was sleeping, and you called me out of the blue. I don't know you. And I don't even know your name."

"Margaret. That is my name. Kiddo. You can close your eyes if you wish. Sure. Go right ahead. But you know that when you awaken, you will be in the mansion. It might be later in the day or whatever. But I will still be here, and I will wait for you when you come over. Do as you wish. Go ahead."

He closes his eyes but reopens them quickly and looks at her. She is lying on the bed smiling. He closes his eyes again and makes a wish. Everything becomes dark and quiet.

A plane is heard flying overhead. A police car is heard roaring down the street. He tosses and turns on his bed. Opening his eyes, he smiles because he is home, and he is safe. He smells himself and realizes that he needs to take a shower.

5

      Alfred got himself together. He had breakfast and he drank two cups of coffee. He washes the dishes and dries them. He sat in the office and surfed the net for the latest news. It began to rain just a bit. The sun came out. He stopped what he was doing for the moment and got off the chair to look out of the window. He smiles as a rainbow appears. He loves rainbows. Heading back to his chair he stops when he hears that phone ringing again. Hesitantly, he heads to the hallway and opens the door. Answering the phone, he does not say a word for the moment.

"I know that you're here because you picked up the phone. How are you?" Margaret asks.

"No," he whispers.

"Yes. I know. Are you feeling better today? How was your rest? Are you rested now?"

"Yes, to all your questions. How are you doing or need I ask?" he wonders.

"I am fine. As I was trying to tell you last night, everyone will continue to talk to you to see if you're the real thing. Long story short, they want money. This is why she was a recluse and did not go out except for the essentials. Everyone needs and want money. She got hers and I got mine. And we both had some before we got married. Many people come into money after marriage or during a marriage. But we already came from money. The way that we both were raised, we were taught not to flaunt the wealth and to be grateful for

what we have. And we did. I wanted to go to church

more but people knew who we were, and they always

looked at us that way. If you know what I mean. Unlike

your friend, Claire, I like sex and I have no problem

admitting it. She was a true lady. She did it now and

then, but she was not one to dwell on it or need it as is

my case. She was a true lady. I'm sure that is one of the

things that she admired about you also. You did not get

her back to your room and try to make out with her. I

know that most men probably would have. Did the

wrinkles bother you about her? Or did you look past

that?"

　　He clears his throat.

　　"I saw a lonely woman who had things on her

mind. She looked sad. And it was apparent that

something was amiss. Were there other men who were after her and wanted to get to her money?"

She laughs and giggles and snorts.

"Sorry. I don't usually snort. Yes. There were men her age and older who were interested in her. But she was not having it. She enjoyed the company and the conversation but that was about it. Are you okay now? Or are you still spacy about all of this?" she wonders, as she sips her coffee.

"Yeah. Uh. Yeah. There's nothing that I can do about it because it is here. It is real. And it is as it is."

"That's good to hear. I really hope that you do get it because it's not going to change. They're here and they will keep coming. That little person, what's her name, Anna? She means well. She really does but look at her. Did she tell you about her boss?"

"Yes. She did. She was upset. She said that she just gave him oral sex."

"Yeah right," she says, laughing. "Please. The girl is smart and highly educated but she got to where she is because of him. He put his dick in her for a minute and it was over. Come on. Some people will do anything for a job and a title for money. But she is a good person. Listen. Listen," she says. "They're after you, and they want some of that money. You're an outsider and you got her money and the pad. You're a good man and smart. Just be careful. Can I ask you something?" she asks, as she continues.

"Sure. Don't stop now," he says, sarcastically.

"I'm being serious. Have you---have you felt something there? Has she come to you?"

"How. How did you know?" he wonders, as his eyes get wide.

"We all possess some talent. She possessed a lot of talents. She came to you before in a vision. Didn't she?"

"Yes. She did. The first time that I was here. I thought that I was going crazy."

"Really?" she asks.

"No. Not really," he admits.

"I didn't think so. Listen. Have you uh---have you explored the house in detail?" she wonders, as her voice drops, and she becomes serious.

"What do you mean?"

"I figured as much. What I mean is, there are many doors and behind the doors are different decorations. And then there is the basement."

"What?" he yells, getting to his feet.

"Oh. You didn't know that there was a basement? Surely you must have figured that if there is the main floor, and the upstairs, there must be a lower part. Right?" she asks, looking around.

"Okay. Now you're getting me freaked out. I think that I am missing something."

"You know I'm right across the street from you. We could be talking to each other face to face and looking at each other directly in the eyes. But I get the feeling that you're ignoring me. Are you afraid of me or something?"

He laughs nervously.

"No. Of course not. It's just that you guys are coming out of the woodwork, and you want to talk to me about the same thing. It's a bit monotonous. You know?"

"Yes. I know. Listen. You can trust me. Really," she says.

"I don't know who I can trust. As I said before I get it. I understand the concern that everyone has but enough is enough. Had I known that it would be like this, I wish she hadn't taken a liking to me. Geez," he says, looking around at the clock.

"Listen. I want to be your friend. I do. Really. Little Miss Anne will not leave you alone. She is going to continue to bother you for two reasons. She is interested in you, and she works for that pig. That pig sells papers, and he wants to get dirt on you. I believe that you need a friend."

"I'm sure I do although I did nothing wrong. But why should I believe that I can trust you?"

"Because you can. I'm not a young thing. And I am no spring chicken. Sure, I have the money and I did plastic surgery and all that. But I am older, and I don't play games like the others. Even sweet thing, Oscar, sure he would like to be your friend and get his hands on some of the money. I call him sweet thing because he acts that way. But he does have a girlfriend. They have been together for a bit. But to me as well as to others he does tend to come across as very feminine," she says, being honest.

He sighs from exasperation and shakes his head. Looking down at the carpet he stares.

"Whatever," he says, softly. "Are we done yet?"

"No! No!" she says, getting to her feet and reaching for a cigarette. "We are not done yet. I am trying to help you. I know, you heard me say that. Don't you want to trust someone?"

He closes his eyes and lets his mind wander. He smiles as he comes up with a plan.

"Yeah. I guess. What do you want me to do?"

"You're there in that big mansion alone. I am here alone in my big mansion. I live across the street from you. You know?" she asks, smiling but also embarrassed by what she just said.

He thinks before he speaks because he does not want to hurt her feelings. But he is honest and has always been an honest person.

"I thought last night that, you know---Okay. I can be your friend, but I hope that you're not up to anything. If you are, I will never speak to you ever again. You can knock on my door or call me all night. I will not answer."

"I am not like that, and I will prove it to you if you give me a chance. Okay?" she says, speaking honestly and hoping that he believes her.

"Listen. I thought last night that I made it clear that I'm not interested in you. Okay. I like sex. I want to make out with a lady. But I was never one for casual sex with anyone. Or to have sex to just be doing it. I believe in the bible, and I know what it says about sex before marriage. But after being married twice I think I better think about doing that again," he says to the point and being honest.

"Well. I don't think that I need to say anything else about the matter on that subject. You will come around. You said that you like sex. Believe me you will

come around eventually. Are we going to continue

talking on the phone or are you going to come over here,

so that I can look at you in your eyes?" she presses.

"God! What is it with you wanting me there in

person?" he asks, getting a bit irritated.

"When you're ready, come over."

After she spoke those words she hangs up the

phone. She heads to her front door and stands behind

the curtains and stares at his door. He cannot believe

any of this that keeps happening. But it is happening,

and it is real.

6

Alfred finished his lunch and is washing the

dishes. He heads to the sitting room and heads to the

bar. He gets a glass, and a bottle of scotch. Opening the

fridge, he gets some ice. Closing the fridge and turning

around he lets out a loud shriek

"What are you so hyped up about? I told you

that I would always be here with you. And I told you to

be careful because they would come. And come they

have especially Margaret. What a character she is,"

Claire's spirit says.

Slowly turning around completely and doing his best not to drop what he is holding; he notices a woman's translucent body sitting on the chaise lounge.

"Are you okay?"

"Huh? Oh uh. Oh," he says, stunned.

"I said are you okay?"

"Oh. Uh. I'm ok," he says, still in shock and in disbelief.

"You don't look it. You look as if you've seen a ghost," she says.

"Oh really?" he says, sarcastically.

"Oh. I forgot," she says, looking at her translucent body. "I'm in between that's why I look like this. But everything is okay. I told you to be careful because everyone would be coming out of the woodwork. Isn't the boss of the local newspaper a piece of work?"

He pours his drink and takes a long swig.

"Yes. He is. Don't forget his little girl that works for him."

"You know. She does mean well. But she is young and impressive. But don't believe her. I know what she told you. But I know that you're smart and you know in your heart that she slept with him. Right? Yuck! What a nasty beast he is. But she has high aspirations, and she wants money. He gave her a lot of dough and a big bonus that many at work don't know about. I'm talking about the bonus on top of the regular one that everyone gets. And my silly neighbor across the street," she says, giggling. "My goodness. She is way out."

"Yeah," he says, sighing. "Poor thing. But she has money, and she is by herself. You can do whatever you want with your money and that is what she did. You can't blame her for that."

"True. But you must admit that she looks pathetic. She has a nice body, but she is in her seventies. But like you said she can do whatever she wants. Now this. I told you to be careful. If I didn't before, I am telling you now. I'm being very serious here. They're jealous of you because they want a piece of the pie. And they don't like you because you're an outsider and you got my money. But the one across the street, Margaret, she inherited her money. Then she married a rich guy who died. She has money but guess what she does not have and has not had in a while?"

"A man," he says, glancing at her on the chair and turning away.

"I know it must be weird for you to see me like this. Sorry. And you're right about her. She is gorgeous for her age, and she has money but no man. She wants someone a bit younger than she and someone who can get it up. Her last husband, he was a bit older, and he could not get it up. But I must give it to her, she never strayed. But she did look. Oh boy did she look," she says, giggling.

He sips his drink.

"Good for her. When will this nonsense end? Or should I ask will this nonsense end?"

"It will. But not now. They will keep digging until they find some dirt on you. But you're a good guy. You might have made some mistakes in your life but you're a good man. It's written on your face. I've made some mistakes during my youth as well. I got involved with the wrong person also. It's called life. It's part of life. I know this is hard for you and weird. I'm sorry."

"Did you know that this would happen like this? Did you know that those wolves would come out with gnashing teeth and foaming at the mouth?" he asks.

"You do have a way with words. Yes. I knew. Of course, I imagined that something like this would happen. Did you think that this would just be another story? What did you expect?"

"I knew that there would be talk especially once the news got hold of it. Is there more that you're not telling me?" he wonders, as he sips his drink and looks at the translucent image.

"There is nothing else that I must tell you. You are black so of course that is going to attract a lot of attention. You do understand that. People need to get over themselves with this ongoing prejudice that exists in their lives. They need to get a life. Everyone is getting older. Many of our heroes and dear relatives are gone now and will never return. We need to learn from the knowledge that they shared with us. That is how we learned from our mistakes. I know that you have learned from your mistakes because it's on your face and in your eyes. You're a good man, Mr. Alfred. I know that eventually you want another woman because you love women. And I'm sure that you also love sex."

He is quiet for a moment before he speaks.

"True. And as the bible says, one should be married before having intimate relations. I agree. BUT. But" he says, softly, "It's not that easy."

"I understand. I told you to be careful, but you let that woman into the house. Now, she has been inside. She means well but she is all about the money. You saw her boss and you get it. You understand and you get it because you are smart. I had no idea that this would turn out as it has. Honest," she says not skipping a beat.

"You mean that? I don't know about that considering that no one knows anything about me. I'm black and you're an older white lady living by yourself in this gorgeous mansion. You were living in this mansion by yourself I meant to say. We met by happenstance at the bar and the rest is history. Too bad I cannot go back and start over," he says, sounding despondent.

"What do you mean? Of course, you know that is not possible. Correct?" she asks.

"Yes. I know. That's why I said that it is too bad that I cannot go back and start over. I wish I could go back to the hotel where we were talking. Were you feeling well when we were together?" he wonders.

"I---was in a place that I did not like being. I was in a place where I was lonely and not happy. It was dark. This place. This is why I entered that bar that night. I needed to shake the shivers off me. It did not work. But I saw you and I saw your face and the hurt that was there. I felt like a failure at my age. Here I was rich and living in this mansion. I thought that I had a good marriage to a nice man. I was a dutiful wife. I was a good mother to a boy that I birthed. But as they say when kids grow up there's no telling which way they will go. He went to college, but he chose the drug route later and had to deal with that. Then, one day it was time for him to go home. When the two of us went back to the hotel I needed that talk. You are a good listener, Mr. Alfred, and you looked at me directly into my eyes. Many people don't do that. I think sometimes that people like you don't realize how special you are. You are special and I am sure that others have told you that before. But you're humble and don't believe them. Right?"

"You're right. My mom always said things like that to me. But she meant well, and I guess she saw something about me or felt something special about me. There were four of us and we're all different."

He sips the remaining contents of his drink and stares into the glass.

"I understand," she says, after his long pause.

"Do you? Will this ever end? What's next?" he asks, trying to remain calm.

"Remember this. You can run as far as you want. You can go to another country, but you must always return home. I know that you would not sell this mansion and relocate elsewhere. Even if you did, someone would find you. Sorry. This is your home now. I hate to sound like a broken record. But just be careful and don't let them get to you. You're a strong person. That---slut will come over here again. Anna. But you must not give in to her as she comes on to you. I told you she is all about money. She is young, intelligent, highly educated and can get any man. But she is about money. She knows what she is doing. The day that she went on the interview with her slob of a boss, she saw the way that he was looking at her. It grossed her out, but she has high aspirations and---the rest is history."

"She said she did not sleep with him," he says, innocently.

"Yeah right! You saw her. She is gorgeous. Right? Of course, she is. What do you think? Really?"

"We were all young once and we did some things. Right?" he asks.

"But did you ever do anything like that? I know you did not. Am I wrong? Did you ever kiss ass for a job?"

"Of course not," he says, as he frowns from the question.

"That is my point. That is my point my dear. I see you here sometimes. I am watching over you when I get the chance. Always."

"Hey uh someone mentioned something about knowing where the bodies are buried. Was that just---," He stops as she interrupts him.

"Don't listen to idle gossip. Please. Some things that people say they say because of jealousy. And they repeat what they've heard over the years. There is no proof. Gossip sucks. Keep your head high and above the clouds."

"That's easy for you to say. You know?" he asks.

Suddenly, it became dark. He looks to his right for a quick moment. When he turns around and faces the other way, he looks for Claire. But she is gone. He presses the button to recline on the chair. Closing his

eyes, he is out like a light.

Now, it is quiet and dark. Stillness fills the room.

The sound of a dog barking slowly fades away. There is

not a sound for a bit. No wind. No Cars. No dogs

barking. No cars driving down the streets. No fire

trucks blaring down the streets. It is eerily quiet.

Slowly, there is the faint sound of a beep. There

is another one. Then, another one. He can hear

something, but he cannot make out what the sound is or

where it is coming from. He can feel someone breathing

on him because the person is close to him. Now, there is

a light that is being shone on his face. That gets his

attention as he slowly opens both eyes.

"Good," the petite Asian woman says, holding

the small flashlight and pointing it at his eyes. "You

gave us quite the scare. Are you here? Earth to Alfred. Earth to Alfred," she says.

"Where am I?" he asks, in a whisper.

"You tell me," she says, backing away from him and looking at him continually in his eyes.

Looking around the room and trying to remain calm, he wonders where he is. Nothing looks familiar to him, so he has no clue where he is. His eyes focus on the petite woman. She smiles widely. She has long black hair, heavy make-up, small hands and fingers, and short legs.

"Who are you?"

"I am Dr. Wong. You are at the hospital but in my office. I am a psychiatrist. You gave us quite the scare. If it weren't for your nosy neighbor there's no telling what would have happened."

"Huh? What? Who?" he asks, confused.

"Your nosy neighbor across the street in that gorgeous mansion of hers. The one who lives directly across the street from yours. She saw you through her binoculars and you looked as if you were passed out. She called you and let the phone ring for a while, but you never picked up. She decided to call the police. They could not wake you up. But your vitals were fine. The paramedics brought you here. After you were checked out then they sent you here. Now then," she says, sitting on a chair opposite the bed, "Why not tell me what is going on?"

Carefully, he sits upright. Dr. Wong presses the button to raise his bed. He smiles nervously. She looks at him intently at his eyes. He looks confused.

"I'm not sure what happened really."

"What is the last thing that you remember?" she asks.

He thinks of Claire, then he lets out a smirk on his face.

"If I told you, you would not believe me."

"You're wrong. I would believe you. You want to know why?" she asks.

"I do," he says, listening to her attentively.

"Because this is your dream. You passed out and now you are in your dream. Does that make sense?" she asks.

"I'm not sure. Say that again. Please."

"You were in that mansion of yours. It used to be hers, that woman. Then she gave it to you in her will after you two met. Yes. Everyone knows the story. You---passed out from the booze. You were brought here to be checked out and all is well. You're in the

hospital sleeping."

"But you said that I was in your office and that

you're a shrink," he says, with a confused expression on

his face.

She laughs.

"Exactly. That is correct. I'm not sure that I

understand why this is confusing to you. Maybe you

should think about this for a minute to gather your

thoughts and come to realize what I just said."

He looks around the room again. He notices a

window and the buildings in the distance that he can see.

Slowly, he turns and looks at Dr. Wong. He takes a deep

breath.

"I'm not getting it. Sorry. Explain this for me.

Please."

"Sure. Okay. I'm sure that like many of us you have passed out before form overindulging. You're in a dream. You're dreaming. That's where you are. You're safe. When you awaken you will be in your mansion as you were before you passed out. I need to ask you a question though. But it doesn't matter much because this is your dream. You kept mumbling a woman's name over and over. Does the name Claire mean anything to you?"

"Huh? Who?" he asks, excited.

"Calm down. Relax. The name Claire. Does that mean anything to you. You kept saying her name over and over."

"Oh," he says, embarrassed.

"Yes?"

"She. She uh---she owned the home. I mean the mansion. I guess I was thinking of her," he says, hesitantly, wondering what is going through the doctor's mind.

"Oh. Right. Where do we go from here, Mister Alfred?"

"Huh? You called me by my first name. How did you know that was my name? Who are you?" he asks, as he begins to panic.

"I told you, silly. This is your dream. I'm one of the characters in your dream," she says, leaning over and getting close to him. "Where do we go from here?"

"I don't know. I'm sick and tired of people coming over to the house or calling me. They all want the same answers. And they all want to know who I am and why me. I'm just a guy. The Lord made my skin brown. I am highly educated. I speak the King's English. I am an honest man. I made some mistakes in my life as most of us have. Sometimes I wish I could go back to a time when I was happy. But I know that is not going to happen and that is not possible. That is who I am."

"I see. I get it. If you had the chance, would you still go to that bar as before and let nature take its course?" she wonders.

"I'm not sure that I follow you," he asks, still confused.

"You're the one who made the statement. I'm just listening to what you said and now I am asking you a question to see how you would answer it. You know that no one can go back in time to a place that they felt comfortable. That is logically impossible, and it will never happen. You need to accept the present and deal

with it. As for those people that keep bugging you, that

is to be expected. They're jealous of you. They want a

piece of the pie even though they're doing just fine

financially. But you're new here. No one has seen you

before. We heard why you came here but that is all that

we know about you. As for your dream it is a dream.

Sometimes when we go to bed at night we dream. When

we wake up sometimes we remember the dream. Other

times we don't. Sometimes the dream seems so real, but

we know that it wasn't real because, it was a dream.

Currently, you're in a dream and it appears real. You

ask many questions. You doubt many things that

happen. Things happen for a reason. Our minds are

incredible. We can think of things and people. We can

make things in our minds. We can create characters and

worlds. We can create places where we control the

action and people. You are frightened because of all that

has happened to you. But what if your life was like it

was before. Would that really make you happy?"

"I don't know," he says, softly. "I'm not sure

about that. I say that is what I want but I wonder. I truly

wonder. I'm not very sure about that."

"Sometimes my dear, we must be careful of what

we ask and wish for. Because as you know, dreams just

might come true. When a dream or wish comes true we

are shocked. We have no idea how to handle it. We

deny that it really did happen. But it did happen. People

come out of the woodwork and beg for handouts. That

makes no sense of course. I understand. I do. I do.

Now then," she says, holding her head down. "Now

then. I know she comes to you because you told me in

your mind. In your conscience. None of this makes any sense to you. You made me because that is what you do as an artist. I get it."

"How do you know who is always on my mind?" he asks, seriously, confused and sounding a bit sad.

"Everyone tosses aside the wrong person. When we get into an argument we say the wrong things. And we react the wrong way. When you meet some people later in life and you get into a relationship with that person, you realize it was a mistake. A terrible mistake. You did that. As they say twenty-twenty is hindsight. We're all human beings. You create worlds where you feel comfortable in. You're an artist. You write and what you write is always on your mind. I know that you want to get on the next plane far away and get away from all of this. But there is no reason to do that because you know someone will always be around watching you. You can run but you cannot hide. Go to your place within your head and have your peace. You need peace. I can imagine how it must be for you being in that mansion and everyone is wondering about you. Just be careful. Always be careful. This you must do. Be careful."

He does not say a word. Slowly, he sits upright on the bed and smiles at the doctor. She holds out her right hand and holds onto his left hand.

"You must think that I am a fool by the way that I am acting," he says, embarrassed.

"I do not. Where you want to go and what you want to do is up to you. Make the most of what you've got. Remember the Lord gave it to you. You are a religious man, and you truly believe in the Lord. Some

verses you have memorized because they have stuck out
to you. Psalm 54 sticks out to you and is important to
you. It applies to you. I know that you know each verse
word by word. 'Save me, O God, by thy name and judge
me by my strength. Hear my prayer, O God; give ear to
the words of my mouth. For strangers are risen up
against me, and oppressors seek after my soul: they
have not set God before them. Behold, God is mine
helper: the Lord is with them that uphold my soul. He
shall reward evil unto mine enemies: cut them off in thy
truth. I will freely sacrifice unto thee: I will praise thy
name, O Lord; for it is good. For he hath delivered me
out of all trouble: and mine eye hath seen his desire
upon my enemies.' This fits you to a tee and this is why
you say it a lot. It is near and dear to you. Be careful.
Always be careful. People are watching you because

they are jealous of you. They have always been jealous

of you. Especially now with your recent riches. And to

show how humble you are, you haven't even spent a

dime of it. No fancy cars. No fancy wardrobes. No

fancy rings. Nothing. I admire you for that. Always

stay humble. Be you. Be who you are and who you

have always been the kind gentleman that you are," she

says, as she stares at his eyes.

Everything becomes dark again. It is still. The

wind has begun to blow outside. Clouds move along the

sky hurriedly. Fog is making its way into the city. Car

horns can be heard in the distance.

Waking up, he is still on his recliner. Looking

around the room he smiles because he is safe. He was

indeed dreaming. He heads down the long hallway and

heads to the front door. He opens the curtains and looks

out. He notices that Margaret is looking at him through

her binoculars.

7

Anna is resting at home and watching nothing especially that is on television. Her landline rings. She stops what she is doing and looks at her phone. Hardly anyone calls her on that phone. Reaching for the remote she turns the television down.

"Hello? Hello?" she asks, nervously.

"Why are you so nervous?" Margaret asks.

"Oh, it's you. I don't know. Not many people have this number. I was surprised that it rang, that's all."

"Yeah right. What about your clients? Don't they have this number, Anna?"

"What the hell?" Anna says, upset. "How dare you. How dare you."

"Oh, knock it off. I know all about you. Please knock it off. It's okay. We all have done things that we regret. By your reaction I can tell that I struck a nerve. I can also tell that you might still be doing that," Margaret says without mincing words.

"Wow. Wow," Anna says, excited, as her face turns red. "What is it that you want?"

"Baby. I am a woman. I am an old woman now. Okay. But I have tons of money and I pay to look good for my age. You'll get it if you get to be my age sometimes. If it is meant to be. Giving the boss oral sex is not the answer. You've got to have pride. What you've done we've been there years ahead of you. Women will always be second fiddle. Always. Now then. What we all are after is finding out information about Mister Alfred. All of us. I'm telling you right here and now that there is nothing to find out about him.

I checked him out thoroughly. He got into trouble years

ago with some girlfriend. But other than that, he is a

good man. If he was interested in you when you threw

yourself at him, surely he would have given in. You're

impressive and a beautiful young woman. You're highly

educated. But never forget, as a woman they hire you

first and foremost because of your looks not because of

your education, or your experience. You make the

company look good. And all the men in the office are

always looking at you. All the men. Never forget that.

Ever!"

Anna sighs.

"Okay. I get it. I understand."

"Do you? Do you?" Margaret asks, as she lights

a cigarette and calms herself. "If you got it then why

were you getting upset when I mentioned your past?

You are what you are. Right?"

"Yes," Anna says, sighing, as she holds her head

down.

"Then why are you upset? What's the problem?

Don't tell me that you're embarrassed by your past. You

did what you did on your own. Correct?" she asks.

"I did. Yes. I did."

"Then, what is the problem?" Margaret asks,

again, smoking her cigarette.

Silence for a bit.

"I---don't like to think about that."

"You don't like to think about that? Oh, I see.

But wait a minute. Isn't that how you got your current

job? Or are you going to tell me that you got the job

based on your experience? Is that what you're trying to tell me?"

"I do have experience and a degree. I would like to think that is why I got the job. Truly," Anna says, innocently..

"And you really think that? Honestly?" Margaret says, sounding firm as she continues to press the issue.

"I would like to think that. But if I were to find out that I got the job based on my looks, at first I would be a bit upset. But later I would realize that is how I got the job," she says, calmly.

"Sweetie," Margaret says, as she takes another drag from her cigarette, "You got the job based on your looks. That's how and why you got the job. You're attractive and you have a nice little ass. Just call it for what it is. You're an attractive young woman and that is why they hired you. I won't even believe what you just said because you gave him oral sex. No one told you to go there. You did that on your own. Correct?"

"Do you have to be so blunt about things?" Anna asks, getting upset, as she is embarrassed thinking of the past. "You can hurt someone's feelings just by the way that you say things."

"I'm sorry. But you need to face the facts and grow some balls. You're too sensitive for your own good. Grow some balls. Okay?" Margaret says, pressing the envelope.

"Yes. Okay. Why did you call me? Might I ask?"

"Oh. Yes. That. I called you to let you know that you need to stop wasting your time. He, Mr. Alfred does not want some young pussy. Okay? He looks well for his age. But sweetie, he is older than you. You threw yourself at him. Before you ask, I can imagine. Yeah, I talked to him, and we talked about you. You're very impressive but he knows that you gave the boss oral sex. He is not stupid. Okay? He knows. Sorry to be blunt but that is me."

"Um. Margaret. You interrupted my night by calling me. What is it that you want?" Anna asks again, politely, trying not to get upset.

"What is it that I want?" Margaret asks, giggling.

"Yes."

Margaret puts out her cigarette.

"He's mine. Okay? He might not come my way yet. But he will. He will."

Now it is Anna's turn to laugh.

"Yeah right. Sweetie, as you say. I don't mean
to be rude but if I wanted him I could get him. I am
younger and more attractive. I don't have to buy my
looks due to being older. Okay? If I wanted him I could
have him."

"Yeah right. If that was the case then why didn't
anything happen when you were over there the other
day? Hmm? Because he did not want you that's why.
Sweetie. He is older. He has been around the block. He
has screwed many women and he has been hurt. He
does not need some little young chick chasing after him.
He can get anyone that he wants if he wants them. Don't
forget, he is a millionaire now. Oh, and don't forget, I
too have millions of bucks as well. We both have
mansions, and we're retired. You go to work every day
and bust your---ass. Probably literally. Do you shake

your ass when you walk too? Or do you show your tits by wearing certain bras to expose them? What is it? Hmm?" she asks, sarcastically.

"I uh don't have to listen to this. I have youth and that is something that you don't have and will never have again. You're old now and you know it. Sure, you keep your weight down. But the other stuff, the face lift, lifting your breasts, the ass lift, that's all fake. You look like all those other fake old dames in Hollywood. That is what you look like. But more power to you. Remember. I have youth. I can get anyone that I want. Okay. You're right. You're right. I know that I can get any job because of my looks. I know this. And when I leave that big fat pig of a boss, I know that I can get another job easily. Okay? I know this. There. Are you happy now?" she asks, breathing heavily.

Margaret laughs.

"Well bravo. Bravo," she says, clapping her hands. "Glad to hear that you finally admitted that. Looks like I struck a nerve. And you're right. I'm old and I bought this new face. Yeah, I have aged spots. My arms are wrinkled and withered from age and the sun. You should be so lucky to live as long as I have. But guess what? The way that your generation is going, you guys live too fast and careless. You guys know about fentanyl, but you continue to smoke it and use it. It's killing you but your generation continues to use it. So many deaths of young entertainers. Very sad. I've said enough. Goodbye but bear in mind my words that I said to you."

"Yeah whatever," Anna mumbles as she hangs up the phone.

Margaret hangs up her phone and giggles. She heads to her front door window and looks out of the curtains. She nearly lets out a fright. Alfred is standing at her door. She heads to the door and opens it.

"It's you," she says, smiling.

"It is."

"I'm sorry. Please. Please. Come in," she says.

As he enters the door she closes it and locks it. She turns around and looks at him.

"Okay," he says.

"Okay what?" she asks, wondering what he is talking about.

He gets close to her and touches her behind. He kisses her and closes his eyes.

"Okay. You're close to my age. Just a bit older. I don't have anyone in my life. You're here and you keep looking at me. You have money and have had money for a long time. I am new at this. I am known as nouveau riche. You want to---then okay. I think that I can trust you so bring it on. If you're not interested please let me know," he says, being honest and getting to the point.

"Of course, I'm interested. I am the one wearing the negligee with nothing on underneath, silly man. What brought this on?" she asks.

"May I sit please?'

"Yes. Where are my manners?" she asks.

He sits on the couch.

"I figure that this nonsense will go on for some time. I'm close to seventy and you're over seventy. I also figure that you're not after me as the others. And I don't think that you're working with anyone to get information about me. I think that you believe me when I tell you that I am nothing but just a guy. Claire and I met as I said. And that's the truth. The other thing is--- well, I don't know anyone here and since you're obviously interested in me---okay why not?"

"Why not what?" she asks, as if she doesn't know what he is talking about.

"Yeah right. Ha. Ha. You and I together. That is if you want to do it. Sex," he says, embarrassed.

"Yes. I know. Silly man. I know," she says, getting close to him.

He holds his head down from embarrassment.

"I don't know what to say."

"Are you embarrassed to be with an older woman who is hitting on you? Or is it because of this whole thing with people wanting to know about you? Or all the above?" she asks, looking into his eyes.

"Yes. The latter," he says. "Was it necessary for you to change your face? Were you getting wrinkles or something?"

"It's called pride and vanity, silly. I have the money, so I said why not? Let's do it. And I did," she says, honest and to the point. "I know. Claire aged naturally. Good for her. Did you like the grey hair?"

"I did. As you said it was natural. She aged naturally. Good for her. I'm not knocking anyone for, you know, if you want to do that and make changes to your body. It's your money so power to you."

"Yes. More power to me," she says, looking at him flirtatiously. "You want to do it here or in the bedroom?" she asks, bluntly.

"Oh," he says, embarrassed. "I uh. I----never gave it a thought."

"You could have fooled me by the way that you looked at me when you came in here. Follow me," she says.

As he follows her down a hallway she presses a button to turn the lights off downstairs. She heads to a room with a chaise lounge. He follows behind her. She takes off her night gown and reveals her pale white body. To his surprise he becomes erect almost immediately. He takes off his clothes and gets close to her from her rear end. He sighs. As he touches her she turns around and gets close to him. She kisses him passionately and pushes him onto the chaise lounge. He breathes heavily as she gets on top of him and grinds back and forth. She touches his penis and puts it into her vagina. He is embarrassed as she moves up and down. Both are getting excited. He closes his eyes and tries to relax. But it is not that easy. It has been a while since he last had sex.

"Don't fight me baby. You said that you wanted to get together with me. Now here you are. I'm not like the others. You will find that out. Relax. You are tense. Relax. Let it go baby," she says, as she continues to move up and down.

He can feel it coming. He is embarrassed having sex with this older woman. But he is a man, and she is a woman who took care of herself, albeit by having cosmetic surgery. Finally, he releases his sperm and they both let out a scream at the same time. Breathing heavily, they eventually calm down. She gets off him and heads to the bathroom to get towels. She returns and hands him a towel while she wipes herself with the other towel.

"Come," she says, as she leads him to the bathroom.

She starts the water and puts bath salts into the water. They get into the tub and relax. Neither says a word. He is more embarrassed than she is. They scrub each other's back and dry themselves off. As she lets out the bath water, he heads to the other room to get his clothes and walks upstairs to her bedroom. He heads to her bathroom to put lotion onto his body. She enters the room soon afterward.

Later, they get into the bed. They are quiet at first. She breaks the ice and turns to look at him.

"Are you okay?" she asks.

"I am."

"Have you ever made it with an older woman before? I mean someone my age who is a few years older than you," she asks.

"No. You have a nice soft body. Cute soft ass too. Love it," he says, honestly.

"Are you sure?'

"Yes. I'm sure."

"Okay," she says, getting on top of him. "There is an expression that goes I know where the bodies are buried. I know where the bodies are buried," she says.

"Oh?" he says, pushing her gently off him.

"Yes. Every city has secrets. And every person has secrets."

"No. Not me."

"Oh? You don't have any secrets that you never want anyone to know about? Honest?" she asks, stunned by his admission.

"True. Yes. We were all young once. What we did in our youth we did in our youth because we were young. Live and learn from your mistakes. It's part of life," he says, being honest and not embarrassed.

"Yes. It is a part of life. Listen. I'm very sorry for all of this. Truly. I mean it. But you must look at it from everyone's perspective," she says.

"Yes. Yes. I know. I know. Okay?" he says, getting testy.

"Relax. Hey. It's me. Okay? I'm not the enemy. I'm not trying to find out anything here. Honest. I just wanted to say that unlike the others, I'm not trying to figure out why she gave you her money. I wanted to say that you need to think about the situation

here. The old lady, I mean Claire. Sorry. She was older

but she looked okay, and her grey hair was always kept

up. I know the story of how you met, but it is a bit

strange. I mean what are the odds that someone goes to

a bar and has a drink, and then in comes this older

woman who has a ton of money, and she strikes up a

conversation with a stranger? One thing leads to another

and you two go back to your hotel and talk. Just talk and

nothing else. Right? Then, a few days later she passes

away in her home. She made a will naming you as the

sole heir. And here you are now, a stranger who is filthy

rich thanks to that kind person. It is quite an incredible

story. Right?"

"Yes. You're right it is. But as you know, it is a true story and that is how it happened," he says, as he stares at the ceiling.

"And now for some weird stuff," she says. "Every city has secrets as I said. And people have secrets. Everyone has a secret or secrets. You say that you don't then I will believe you. The fat man who owns the newspaper---he had it all. I mean he had a good wife. She is pretty but he is a dog. I don't know whether he has always been that way, but he is. A big fat pig. They have a daughter, but the ex-wife makes sure that the daughter never sees her daddy. If she wants to wifey can't stop her because the daughter is grown now. But when she found out about the truth about her daddy as she got older, she understood why they broke up. She lives quietly here in Seattle with some guy. She stays low key unlike other rich kids. And before you ask

about little miss cutie pie, Anna, let me tell you. She is

bright and highly educated. But she has those looks.

Looks that most men would kill for to get into her pants.

And since he is the boss, if she were to complain about

sexual harassment, well---she is sleeping with the

enemy. Her boss. Oh, sure there were other guys that

she dated. But they were just other guys that she went

out with to the movies and dinner and to just hang out.

Nothing more. She was careful not to drink too much

and pass out or do drugs and get loaded. But the boss

took a liking to her. The rest is history."

"So, what are you saying?" he wonders.

"She does what he wants, and he pays her well.

Not only does she satisfy him sexually even though he

has a pencil dick, but she also works hard and makes the

newspaper look good. This is why he makes sure that

she is given a handsome salary. Poor thing. She knows

better but like I said, with that body of hers---that goes

without saying."

"Is she happy with herself?" he asks, frowning.

"What do you think? You saw her. Right? You

tell me."

"There was something about her that was amiss.

She appeared sad for some reason. I'm sure it's not

because I did not have sex with her. There is something

there deeply that concerns her. You know the weird

thing that I have learned over the years? I have learned

that many gorgeous women over the years are very

unhappy. I noticed this with my mom. She was a

gorgeous woman with makeup on. She always had a

nice figure. But she always got together with men who

were not professional. They worked and they went out,

but I knew that it was only about sex. I would say that

she was happy in her life at times. But not happy a lot in

her lifetime. She deserved better but she made her bed.

When I started dating, I would look at people. I get it

now and understand. But for a long time, I did not

understand why these gorgeous women were with these

rough and tough hard looking men. But that is what they

are used to, probably due to daddy, so they look for that

kind of man. Whatever floats their boats. People think

that I am soft because I don't look or act like a thug. But

I like me and how I am. We are who we are. Either you

have class and education, or you are hardcore and

thuggish."

"Exactly! Exactly!" she says, excitedly, as she turns on the lamp and reaches for a cigarette and lights it. "You don't mind if I smoke do you?"

"It's your house babe. I have been surrounded by secondhand smoke a lot over the years, and I am still here," he says, smiling.

She takes a long drag of the cigarette then puts it out. Opening a drawer, she reaches for a mint. She unwraps it and places it into her mouth. It becomes eerily quiet momentarily. He stares at the ceiling. She glances at the ceiling then at him. She studies his face. His moustache is full of grey hair. He has a small mouth and red lips. His nose is long. He has high cheek bones. For a man his hands are small.

"Yes. You are still here and still a man," she says, reaching underneath the covers and touching his manhood. You know they will continue to hound you

and check you out. They are envious of you and the

money. Don't try to go away anywhere because

someone will always be looking for you no matter what.

The other thing that people are concerned about you is if

you dig into the past."

"The past? Whose past?" he asks, innocently.

"Her past. I know that you don't care but---there

is a past and there are secrets that she took to the grave.

There were----lovers just like you. She was different

and did not care what people thought of her when she

dated men of other nationalities and colors. Maybe that

is what attracted her to you. I don't know. There was

one---brother who she was seeing for just a bit. But that

did not last long. He was a student, but he changed and

got caught up with material things. She gave him a car

and that raised a ruckus. But that all died as soon as it began. He was okay. He barely graduated but he did. He lived there with her for a while, but no one knows where he is now."

"Are you saying that she likes black men or young black youth?" he wonders, looking at her face.

"No. But it was odd that someone of her ilk would do such a thing. You know? I mean I would never date a much younger man than myself. You're about my age so here we are. You get it?"

"Yes. I do. Where do you play in all of this?" he asks. That catches her off guard.

"What do you mean?'

"I mean here we are in this position. You have been watching me for Lord knows how long. Where do you play in all of this?" he repeats his question.

"Like Claire, I am just an older woman who lives in a big mansion all by herself. That is me nothing else. Yes, it can be a pain living here alone and cleaning this place. But it can also be fun too. I try to make it fun and take my time and put on some music or a movie."

"Where do you fit in all of this?" he asks, again, catching her off guard.

"What do you mean?"

"Just like I said. I know what you said about not being like the others and trying to figure me out. But where do you fit in all of this?" he repeats his question once more.

"Sweetheart. I told you. Yes, I watched you because of what happened. I check you out because I am here by myself and so are you. I know that little Anna was nothing to you. You don't come across to me as someone who is interested in some young pretty thing. Now, I may be wrong. But you don't come across like that to me. Am I right?" she queries, as she anticipates his answer.

"You are right. As I always say, let the other dirty old men go after the young girls. I look of course. But no, I am not interested in a young girl or even a young woman for that matter."

"Listen. I need to get serious with you," she says, sitting upright in the bed and looking at Alfred. "This house---I mean your house has a basement. People don't like to go down into basements for various reasons. If you've seen horror movies then you know what I'm talking about."

"I do. But what are you talking about the mansion? There's a basement down there?" he asks, confused.

"Yes. I take it that you've never explored the house fully. You should. You need to. If you're not interested then don't do it. As you know, there are a lot of doors. A lot of doors."

He sighs and is quiet momentarily before he says another word.

"Are you purposely trying to frighten me?" he asks, nervously as he manages a nervous smile.

"No. I'm just being honest. You're safe there. Whenever you want to get away, you can go into one of the many rooms."

"What are you saying? Will you just come right out and be open with me?" he asks.

"You're safe there. Very safe. It's a safe house.
The entire house is safe. It cannot be penetrable."

"But why?" he continues to press, hoping that he
can get honest answers from her.

"All houses and mansions have secrets."

"Oh. We're back to that again," he says,
sounding exasperated.

"Yes. We are," she says, softly as she gets close
to him.

"What are you saying? Listen. You seem as if
you're on the level with me. I might be wrong, but I am
willing to take a chance," he says.

"Oh?" she says, shocked.

"You're a mature woman. You have money. I
don't think that you play games. Games are for young
people. Please just be straight with me and tell me

what's going on. Sometimes I wish I had never met her
if I knew that things would end up like this," he says,
exasperated and disgusted.

She holds her head down for a moment. She
sighs. Then she turns and looks at him.

"It's all very simple. They want the money.
They want some of the money because she had no heirs.
Everyone knows that. You came along out of the blue
and now you have it. The boss is an asshole. He is a big
fat pig. That girl---is young. She is smart but young.
Many men cannot stand her because of how she is. She
knows that she is gorgeous, but she shoves men away.
They get upset and they don't like that. When she first
got here she dated a guy but only for a short time. She
let him sleep with her once but that was it. But when it

comes to money she sleeps with that big fat pig. Thank goodness you did not fall for her schemes."

"What do you mean?" he asks, looking startled.

"Oh, come on Alfred. I mean just as I said. Had you slept with that girl something would have happened. She would have accused you of sexual harassment or something and that would have been it. You just watch. Eventually when things aren't cool with her she will say that big fat pig raped her. As for the others they just want to see what you are up to. They won't admit it, but they know that you're a good man and a good person. All that one must do is look at you. Some people are evil looking and are evil and mean. But not you. I'm sure that you know that, but you won't admit that to yourself. Right?"

"Yes. You're right," he says, softly as though he were embarrassed.

"Why is that? You have a lot of hidden emotions and hurt within yourself. Of course, it involves a woman. Or a few women. Right?"

"Yes. Two. One who I should never have gotten involved with. The other I should have never let go. Before you ask. Yes, she was my first love and will always be my first love. No matter what successes and monetary gains that I have in my life. She will always be my first love. Each night for years on end to this day I pray for her safety and that she is happy. I never knew that she was the one for me until I let her go. I tried to get back with her. I apologized to her. I asked to come back home, she hesitated but then she said no. I called her once after that. Then, no more. I let her go. I left her alone. Thanks to the internet I looked her up. I know where she is. I found her telephone number. But I left it alone. It is as it is and where it needs to be," he says, trying not to get emotional.

She reaches for his right hand and squeezes it.

"I'm sorry. I know the feeling. My husband was a cheater later in our marriage. I wonder if he was always a cheater. He married me for my looks and was happy with me. That's what I thought anyway. Maybe too much information but he was not good in bed. He could barely last long and he did not have a big one, if you know what I mean. That did not bother me. It was as it was. He was all about business and money. That is all that he thought about most of the time. He figured that we should be happy where we were in life and where we were living. I was happy so I let it be and did not complain much. And I knew that it would not have done any good had I complained."

"What happened to him?" he presses the issue without being aggressive.

"Dead from a heart attack. Only sixty-three when he died. But he worked like a dog. I've been in here ever since. I was a dutiful wife. Honest. I had a chance to get with---a boy. He was much younger than me. But I knew that I would never forgive myself. I let him go and that was the end of that. Sorry. We got off the track of what we were talking about. I am here to find everything that I can about you. We all are. The police checked you out. You're a good man. You made one mistake in your life but we're all human. There is nothing to tell anyone about you. Nothing. But they will not give in until they see you make a mistake. Silly, huh?"

He laughs. He turns and faces her.

"I know that you're silly but that makes absolutely no sense in the least. That is idiotic. What happened with the two of us is the truth. Hell. What do those people want me to do give them hand outs? Geez. My goodness already," he says, getting upset.

"No. No!" she says, putting her hand over his mouth. "Don't you dare do that. Don't ever do that. That is what they want you to do. Lose it. You're better than they are. And you're bigger than they are too. You're different and they know that. They see you and they know that you're not like the rest. You're a highly educated man. You are a proud black man. Good for you. Stand tall and walk proud. That is what you do.

You're special. I promise that I will not be like them.

They will approach me and want to know if I found out

anything about you. I did not. As you said, we are older

and wiser. There is no need to play games. I know that

you probably want to run and go somewhere far. I don't

blame you. But you know someone will be following

you always. Silly, I know."

"So, the game is afoot and will always be afoot.

Right?" he asks.

"See? I have never heard anyone speak like you.

Wow. The game is afoot. Sherlock Holmes all the way.

How funny! It'll be okay. I promise," she says, looking

into his eyes.

8

They fell asleep in each other's arms. Eventually, they let go of each other and slept peacefully on each side of the bed. She sleeps quietly but snores now and then. He only snores when he is very tired. A few hours passed since they went to sleep. He hears a low sound of a bell in the distance. Tossing and turning he continues to sleep. There it is again, ringing softly. Slowly, he opens his eyes and glances at Margaret. He sees her lying on her right side. He smiles. Then…he feels someone touch him on his right shoulder. He wants to let out a shriek. Slowly…he turns around. Claire's spirit is standing over him with her right indexed finger over her mouth.

"I put her into a deep sleep. She is okay. I haven't much time. We've been busy up there. Be careful with her. I know what she said to you and what she told you. Be careful. You know nothing about her. You only know what she told you. Be careful and be yourself. I knew that it was only a matter of time before she got with you. That's okay. I'm not knocking you. Believe me, I understand. As they say man does not live by bread alone. I get it and understand it. Be careful my love. You are my love in case you did not realize that. I saw something in your eyes that night at the bar. You saw sadness in my eyes."

"I don't get it. I still don't get it," he says, sighing. "I want to go back. I need for this to stop. I'm confused."

"I'm sorry. I am very sorry. Truly. But you cannot go back, and you know that. Our minds are powerful and very real. In your mind, perhaps at night, you can go back. But this is only in your mind. And when you awaken it will be the present. You will awaken and you will be here with her," she says, looking at the woman sleeping soundly in the bed.

"Did you know that this would happen?"

"I did not. But I am not surprised that it has happened. Look at the source and the whole situation. But I am very sorry. Truly," she says.

"What if---what if I donated lots of money? Would that make a difference?"

She laughs.

"You're not serious. I know that you are not serious. It would not make a difference because of you.

I know I keep sounding like a broken record. But here you are a stranger in town. You have not been here for long, and you meet me in the bar. Of course, it was innocent, and everyone is aware of that. But you're not a local. That is what is killing everyone. You are not a local. They know that you're a good guy and that you have a kind heart. All that they must do is look at you and see that. Some people are ugly and mean and hard to look at. Not you. Now," she says, glancing at Margaret, "You're here with her. That will make them realize that you're normal. We all have our needs. She does not need anything from you. Well----you know what I mean. I hate to be nasty, but you know. You gave her what she needed. And I would gather that you wanted that too. Right?"

"I did. It was okay. It turned out a lot better than I would have imagined. She has soft skin," he says, still uncomfortable speaking to a translucent spirit.

"Sorry, I look like this. You're going to be okay. I'm sorry," she says, holding out her right hand.

"Yeah. Right."

He holds his head down and glances at Margaret. He has a sense of calm thinking of her for a change. He did not know what to think at first with her calling him and talking to him. But for once, he begins to think that perhaps she is a good person and a good soul.

"Yes. Yes. I see it there on your face. You like her after all. Good for you. But as I have told you several times, be careful. Wherever you go there will always be eyes on you. That big fat pig of a boss of the newspaper, he will never let this go. Oh no. He will keep sending that girl over here. She will want to be

friends with you. But we know what she is after. She

will throw herself at you, but she will get the message

that you are not interested in her. Even if you give her

some money, she will continue to dig and dig. Poor

thing. She is young. Highly educated. Has a brain on

her. But she wastes her time on that big fat pig of a

boss. Why? She says it is about money, but I wonder.

He is nothing but a pig. Sure, she gets to write for the

newspaper. But what about pride? And what about

class? What about class? You, my friend. My beautiful

friend, you have class. You are intelligent. Highly

educated with a brain on you. You are very intelligent.

That is the other thing that bothers them about you. You

are black. You are strong and you are highly intelligent.

They act as if they have never been around anyone like

that. But we know that is nonsense because that big fat

pig has attorneys. And some of them are of different

races. Everything will be okay. But you just do not and

will not believe any of this. Will you?"

He sighs.

"How can I?"

"Okay. Let me ask you something. Okay? You

believe in God. I see a few of your books that you have.

You are a believer. Don't you believe that everything

that has happened is due to the Lord?" she asks, looking

at him.

He is stunned to hear her ask him that question.

"Of course, I believe in the Lord. I just don't

believe that---you know---be careful what you ask for

because you just might get it."

"And you got it. You finally got it. Right? There are many people that would love to be in your shoes. Let it be and just accept it. Just accept it. What is it? Please. Tell me. What is it?" she implores him, as she glances at Margaret tossing and turning.

It is a while before he says anything. Slowly, he gets out of the bed and heads to the window. He looks out of the window at the darkness. He does not say a word. The wind makes it presence. He smiles. Turning around, he heads towards Claire's spirit. He sits opposite her on a chair.

"I don't know what to believe. What are the odds of what happened, would happen that night when we met at the bar? What are the odds of something like that happening?"

"I understand. I do. But you know what your problem is. Your problem is that you question things. Rather than accept them you question them. I understand but you must let it be. Just let it be. You are a believer. I see your glow on your face. I feel your spirit. I feel the positivity in you. You are a good soul and someone who many would like to be with. There is no one like you. You do not want to accept this but it's true. Every word that I say to you. Now this one before you, Margaret, she means well. But in the beginning, she was like the others. She wanted to know why you and why not someone else. They all want to know where you came from. They know the answer to that because they checked you out. But they will not let it go. Ever. They will continue to dig and dig, and they will look like fools because you have been honest about everything. Oscar knows that you are sincere. He

always smiles like that. But he knows that you are

sincere. You ever notice that he has not bothered you.

Unlike the others he has not bothered you once."

"Yeah. He's a funny guy and he appears as

though he is a good man also. If I close my eyes and

reopen them will you still be here?" he asks.

"I should still be here unless you're thinking of

going back to where we were in the hotel. If you do this

I guess it will make you happy. Is that it?" she asks.

"You already know the answer to that. You

already know the answer to that."

"You refuse to accept what is before you. He

gave it to you. He made it happen. You know who I

mean. I told you what will happen after you go there.

The mind is powerful and creative. Do what you must if

this will make you happy. Always remember this: no matter how much in denial you are, what is before you is real. We met by chance. I did not set out to meet you. We met on that cold evening at the bar. Go back there if you must. If you must. If you must. I will be there, and I will always be here with you. Forever," she says, as everything slowly fades to black.

It is quiet for a few minutes. Then lightning lights, the night sky. This causes the patrons to shriek from laughter. He glanced at the bartender briefly.

"Are you okay over there, sir?" the petite female bartender asks, smiling politely.

"Yes ma'am. I am fine," Alfred says.

"You don't look fine. Is there anything wrong?" the bartender presses.

"No," he says, looking at himself and his clothes.
He stares at the cocktail glass that is before him. Taking
a sip, he notices an older woman coming into the bar.
She is older and alone. She has on a full-length coat.
She sits at a table. The bartender comes over and the
older lady orders her drink. Alfred tries his best not to
look at her but that is easier said than done. She looks at
him and their eyes meet. She smiles politely at him. He
can see sadness on her face and sadness in her eyes. Her
skin has wrinkles. But looking at her he can tell that
once upon a time she must have been an attractive
woman. The bartender gives the woman her drink. She
hands her a twenty-dollar bill. She heads back to tend
the bar. Sipping her drink, she places the glass onto her
table and stares at the glass. Alfred smiles. She notices
him smiling and motions to him if it is okay for her to sit

at his table. He nods his head. Getting off the chair, the gentleman that he is, she heads over to his table and sits opposite him.

"I'm Claire and you are?"

"Alfred," he says, shaking her hand and then sitting on the chair.

"Déjà vu," she says.

"What's that?"

"Déjà vu," she repeats.

"Oh? How so?" he asks innocently.

"Here. Now. Us. Together. In this bar. At this table on this cold rainy night. Have we met before?" she wonders.

"I don't think so. I just came here. I'm moving to Anchorage. Time for a change. And time to get away from the heat. I'd rather be in a city where it is cold most of the time than suffer in the heat. I'm from California. I'm by myself now and I always wanted to move to Alaska for the cooler weather. I must get used to the winter with all that snow though," he says, smiling.

"Has anyone ever told you that your face glows?"

"Yes. Mom of course and other people also. I guess it's always been there. Do you live near here?' he asks.

"Oh. That's right. You're not from here," she says, laughing. I'm what you might call old money. I've lived here for years. I've been single for years now. I live in one of those big mansions. But I don't want to talk about that. Are you staying at the hotel up the street from here?"

"Yes. I am. It's nice and quiet. I like it like that. Quiet and peaceful. That is what I am used to. That is what has been missing far too long from my life. Peace and quiet. Now, thank the Lord, I have it. We don't know how much time we have left here on Earth. We must make use of it while we are here. The time."

"You look young, but your moustache is grey. Are you in your sixties?" she asks.

"I am indeed," he says, smiling. "And I would say that you are in your seventies. You look great. And I love your grey hair. Good for you. Many people dye their hair. But I like it natural. Good for you," he says, smiling.

"Hey. Can we uh--- can we get out of here? Please?"

"Sure," he says.

They finish their cocktails. He leaves a tip, and they head out the door. She follows him to his hotel room. They step into the hotel. The young woman behind the desk smiles at him. He and Claire get onto the elevator and look straight ahead as the doors close. No one says a word. The elevator takes them swiftly to the fifth floor. The elevator stops. The doors open. She gets out first. They walk together side by side and he stops in the middle of the hallway and pulls out his card key. He walks into the room and turns on the light switch. After she enters, she closes the door and locks it. They stand in the middle of the room and look at one another. She looks around the room and smiles.

"This is nice. Very nice," she says.

Before he can say a word, she touches his face. She caresses his face. He smiles but it is a nervous smile.

"Uh---please. Let me take your coat."

He helps her with her coat. He hangs it up in the closet. He looks around the room and sits on a chair. She lies on the bed and stares at the ceiling.

"Are you okay?" he asks.

"Yes. Please. Sit next to me. Lie with me on the bed. Please," she says.

He acquiesces and lies next to her on the bed. They are both lying on the bed together with their clothes and shoes on.

"It has been sometime since I have been with anyone. My husband has been gone for a while. He was a jerk. I tried to find the goodness in him. But the bad part was always there. I could have met anyone if I

wanted. I have gone to that bar several times. But I

never wanted to meet anyone. That is until now. I

thought that now, tonight was as good of a time as any to

go out and have a drink, and perhaps meet someone.

And that is what I did and here we are. You're a good

person. You have good karma. Like me, you have been

hurt. It shows on your face, what's your name again,

Alfred?"

　　"Yes. Alfred. You are right. I tend to give my

heart too easily and to the wrong person. I should have

stayed with my first wife. She was the one for me.

Hindsight is twenty twenty as the old saying goes. But

through it all, the sadness, the drinking, the crying, the

depression, we continue. We go on. We thrive. We

must hold our heads up and continue. Not give in to

defeat. And not let defeat or loss take hold of us. We know that we are good people, and most of the time it is not us but them. The other people. They are the bad people. The evil people. They are users. We are honest and admit to ourselves of our weakness. But it takes two, always two, to make a relationship work."

"Yes. How very true. I can attest to that. It sucks when you marry young. You live together and everything is great and fun. You're getting along together. But later people and situations change. Live and learn from your mistakes. Divorce is not the answer but so many of us, me included, think that is the answer. To some it is the answer to a permanent solution. But some of us, like myself, know that was not the correct solution. We might have thought so at the time but looking back at the situation years later, we know that was not the answer. Sure. You get over it through the

years. You meet new people. Some you might have a

serious relationship with, and it lasts for a while. But

you never forget the first person that you were with.

And you never forget your first love," he says, sounding

sentimental. "And you? Are you in the same boat?"

"Of course," she says, laughing. "Of course.

People are funny. People put on a good face. Some

mask their feelings by going out to bars with friends.

Others flirt with women and try to act normal. Then,

there are those who fool around with people from work.

Bad news. Very bad news. Everyone hurts. Married

couples. Single couples. And especially married

couples who have kids. It takes a lot to have kids. A lot.

Did you ever want kids?" she asks.

"I did. The wife did not. I thought that she would change her mind. Wrong. I changed my mind the older that I got. But the way that society has gotten over the years, I'm glad I never had kids. The world is such a violent place now. The world. This world. The cities. This city."

He stops talking for a moment. The wind howls outside and causes the lights to flicker. She glances to her right at the window to look at the wind through the curtains. But the dark curtains block the window.

"Dreams. Wishes. We all dream, and we all have dreams. Wishes. Some say they come true. Some say they do not come true. They come true because people play the lottery, and someone wins. Crazy. What are the odds? Out of this world. What are some dreams that you have, Mr. Alfred?" she asks, looking at him.

"To be happy. To have peace. To be financially set. To not have drama and to have a quiet place somewhere alone. I love women and I miss having a woman with me. But I hate drama. I don't do drama. Drama sucks. You know? And what dream or dreams do you have?" he asks.

"My dreams came to fruition at a young life. Both parents were highly educated and had good jobs. I went to great universities and received a master's. I got a good job. And I met my future husband one day in the same building. He sucked in bed. He just wasn't any good. We were together for many years, but we divorced. I never was seriously involved with another man. I met some men, and we went out to dinner and the symphony. But it was nothing serious. They were my age but looked older because of their jobs. They smoked and drank and put on weight. I was satisfied

with being by myself. But I did miss being with

someone and going to different places together. I found

black men to be intriguing and interesting. But I never

acted upon it until I saw you tonight. There's something

about you, Mister Alfred. Your face is a glow, and you

seem like a sincere person. Honestly and truthfully.

That's the truth."

"Thank you," he says, softly.

She reaches for his right hand. They hold hands

and look at one another. He looks at this woman's

wrinkled face that once was beautiful. She has a nice

smile, but her eyes tell the whole story about her life.

She peruses his face as well. He does not have any

wrinkles, but she sees sadness behind his eyes. His face

is blank with no blemishes. Hard to believe that he is in his late sixties, but he is. They both close their eyes.

"You know no matter where you go to in your mind, you must always come back to the present. We all want to get away from reality for a while. We must do this sometimes. But in the end we must come back. If we do not come back we will become lost and lose reality. This is why I envy writers and artists. They go to worlds that they create. They stay there but they come back to reality because they know they must face reality. It's as you said you want to be alone and have peace because you need peace. It's no fun to have drama in one's life. Drama sucks. You know?" she says.

"I do. But what do you mean by we must come back to reality when we dream?" he queries her.

"We can go to any place where we want when we want. We go there because reality sucks. But we must return because if we don't we become lost, in our dreams, in our fantasy. You know what I mean, right, Mister Alfred? I know that you do."

"Yes. I know what you mean. And you know. Sometimes I wish I could just exist and have it where not many people would know me. I hate drama and I want to be alone. But for whatever reason people flock to me. Weird. I love women and sex, so that will always be a part of my life. But the bible has strong feelings about having sex when you're not married. Issues, issues, issues. If I truly believe in the bible as I say, then I am not supposed to have premarital sex."

"You're a good soul. You know that? Really. You are," she says, closing her eyes.

"That's what they tell me. I try. And I always try to be a good person," he says, falling asleep.

Margaret wakes up to use the restroom. After washing her hands, she turns and looks at Alfred lying on the bed. Turning off the bathroom light she heads back to the bed. She reaches for a bottle of water and takes a couple of sips. Getting back into bed she glances at Alfred.

"Of course, you're special. Silly. Why would you think otherwise?"

"What?" he asks, still groggy.

"You said that you try to always be a good person and a good soul. You are. I told you it shows on your face. It's who you are. It is on your person."

"What are you talking about?" he asks, confused.

"You know. I heard you talking. Of course, no one is here. But you were talking to---her. Weren't you?"

"I must have been dreaming," he says, innocently.

"Uh huh. You probably were. But I know that she speaks to you. She had a strong spirit. She believed in ghosts, souls, and spirits. I can imagine that you do as well. Right?" she wonders.

"I do. Listen. This needs to end. This whole thing with people, you know, checking me out to find out about me. Crazy," he says, sighing, and then yawning as he stares at the ceiling.

"I told you. The big boss will not rest. He will not leave this alone. Ever. He is a newspaper man, and he wants to get the goods on stories before others get it.

I believe every word that you tell me. But he is not like that, and neither is sweet, little Ann. I'm sorry. Truly. I am sorry."

"Yeah. I wonder," he says, still groggy.

"Hey. What is that supposed to mean?" she says, as she reaches over and turns on the light. Her sheer nightgown exposes her nude body. "Well?" she says, getting angry, as she folds her arms.

He glances at her.

"How am I supposed to know that you are who you really are? And how am I supposed to know that you're sincere and not like the others? Huh?"

"You don't. But after talking to me and--- sleeping with me, I know that you don't feel that honestly in your heart. I know that you might still have some doubts. But I know that you believe me. I know you do. If I'm wrong tell me. Please," she says, touching him on his right leg.

He does not say a word because he knows that she is a good person and sincere. He looks at her pale face and eyes. He manages a smile.

"I'm sorry. You are a good person. I know that. I'm just sick of this whole charade. Maybe that is not the right word to use. But I'm sick of this whole affair of me being here and people prying into my life. I get it as I said. But come on, it's been a while now. I'm here and I am who I am. As for that girl, nothing makes sense with her. She is there working for him trying to get information. But I am not interested in her young skinny butt."

Margaret giggles.

"You know that when she finds out that we're together, she's going to flip. She's young and fine but you're here with me. You know that she's going to flip because of that. Right?"

"I couldn't care less. Truly," he says, yawning and lying flat. "I only know that I'm a good person. When I got into trouble when I was younger I knew better. And I knew that eventually I would grow up and come back to the bible. I was raised like that. I'm a good person and I've always known that."

She turns off the lamp and snuggles next to him as they go back to sleep. A faint light shines in the hallway before it goes off.

9

The next day. Anna always gets into the office earlier than the others. The newspaper industry is cut-throat. Everyone wants to get the latest scoop before the next person so that he/she gets the byline and the credit. Anna heads to her desk and takes off her coat. For once, she does not have on a short dress. She has on a pair of pants and a sheer top. Although she has on a bra, the top is sheer, and you can see the top of her big breasts. The big boss loves looking at her breasts. He already made it to the office and had his coffee and donut. He made a few calls and had yelled at a few of his contemporaries. He calls her on her office phone.

"Yeah?"

"I'm here and so are you. No one else is here. So, what gives?" he asks, pacing his office.

"I'm here. I am getting organized if that is okay with you."

"Yeah. Yeah. Just get in here soon," he says, slamming the phone down.

One of the older women comes into the office. She smiles as she acknowledges Anna. She wants to say something to Anna about the big boss. But she knows better so she just heads to her desk and gets organized as she takes off her jacket and cap. As the lady heads to the coffee room, Anna heads to the big boss' office. She knocks on the door. He gets off the chair and heads to the door. She glances at him. His face is sad and red. She can tell that he is in a mood. He closes the door and the curtains. She sits opposite him facing his desk.

"Oh. No hand job?" he asks.

"Really?"

"Really," he says.

She rolls her eyes and heads towards him.

"You know I keep you happy here. And I give you more money than most people in the office. Right?" he asks, looking at her face that has on a ton of make-up.

"Yes. You're always right," she says.

"Good. Then please stop rolling your eyes," he says, reaching for the box of tissues in his desk drawer.

She unzips his pants and rubs her right hand on his business. It doesn't take him long to get excited. She feels embarrassed but she has done this for him several times before. And he is correct. He takes care of her financially. She is a bit embarrassed as he ejaculates on her hand. He pounds his desk and turns red. He hands her the box of tissues. She wipes her hand. She leaves his office to wash her hands thoroughly. As she returns from the restroom and heads to his office, the older woman stops her.

"Why? Why do you do---why sweetie?" she asks.

"Why? You were young once. Right?" she says, whispering into the woman's ear.

"I was. Yes," the woman says.

Anna heads to the big boss' office. His face is still red. He looks pathetic and sad. She looks at him and smiles politely. But he is sad to look at. He might be the big boss and have a ton of money. But within his soul he is a sad, unhappy soul. She sits on a chair and crosses her legs. This turns him on. He has always been in awe of her beauty and her legs. He gives her that look of his and she knows what that means. She gets off the

chair and heads towards him. He is breathing heavily.

"Are you okay? You look flushed," she says,

sarcastically.

"Yes. Yes. Whoop! I'm fine. I'm fine! Yes!

Wow," he says, giggling.

As he tries to contain himself. There is a knock

on the door.

"YES!" he yells.

"Sorry to bother you, boss. There are two people

here to see you," the older lady, Betty says, as she moves

to the side.

The big boss and Anna both have shock and

disbelief on their faces. They can't believe it. Standing

in front of them now in the office are Margaret and

Alfred.

"Oh. Uh. Please. Please. Have a seat," he says.

The room smells like sex. We all know what that scent smells like. The big boss still has a grin on his face.

"I am sure you know who we are. Let's get this out into the open. Shall we?" Alfred says. "I don't know what you hope to find about me, but you're wasting your time. I get it and I understand how you feel. Out of the blue here come this man that no one knows anything about. He meets one of the richest women in Seattle in a bar. A few days later she passes away in her sleep. And she leaves this man, a stranger, millions of dollars. Believe me I understand your curiosity but that's the way it happened. I was in the bar having a scotch and soda. She came in soon after and we made eye contact. She looked sad. She asked if she could sit by me, and I told her yes. We talked about adult stuff and life. After a few minutes she said that she wanted to go to my room. We finished our drink hurriedly and we went to my room. There was no sex. I don't think that I even kissed her. As I said, we both had issues and it was obvious on our faces. It's called life. We chatted for a while, and then she left to go home. I had not heard from her in a few days. After the second day, all hell broke loose. The flood gates flew open big time. But I am sure that you know the rest of the story after that. And that's how it went. There is nothing to it. Later, I met Oscar who came to the house and introduced himself. Then we went to the bank, and I got over the initial shock and that was it. That gorgeous mansion was mine. Then your---worker here came over. We talked a bit and drank champagne for a bit. She passed out. She woke up and that was it. This beautiful woman here is

my neighbor. I am sure that you know her no doubt.

She came over one night and talked to me. Yes. We're

seeing one another as I am sure that you know by now."

"Yes. We see that," Anna says, angrily, sizing

up Margaret. "You got lots of money now. What are

you doing with her?"

"She is nice, and she is the only person who I can

trust and believe. All you other people are weird and

strange. Very strange. You're a beautiful young

woman, Anna. But you're doing what other young

woman have done before you. Selling yourself short. I

understand and I get it. But you deserve more. Don't

you have scruples about yourself? I don't mean to be

blunt. But you know what I mean. Right?" he asks.

Anna holds her head down. She is embarrassed because she knows that Alfred is correct. The big boss is leaning back on his chair as he digests everything that has been said. He opens a drawer and reaches for a cigar. But he does not light it.

"You're right. I know," Anna says, softly, in a whisper, wiping her eyes.

"Jah. Jah. Jah," the boss says. "You listen to me," he says, pointing at Alfred. "I don't care where the hell you came from. You got that? But I want to tell you something. We're all pissed because we know that there was no one in her life. Not even a distant cousin. If there is such a person we never heard about it. We knew who she was, and we knew that she lived in that big, beautiful mansion alone. And then one day, damn it!" he yells, as he pounds his desk, "You come along!

You! Why you? Huh? Why you?" he asks, foaming at the mouth. He reaches for his handkerchief in his back pocket and wipes his mouth.

"Do you hate anyone who is not Caucasian? Is that it?" Alfred casually asks.

"No. No," Anna quickly adds, looking at the boss. "He's just a jerk. That's all. Trust me. He loves all women including black women, but they would not put up with him."

The boss' face is beat red. He tries his best to calm down but that is easier said than done. Anna manages a smile as she glances at Margaret and Alfred. They smile politely and get off their seats and head to the door.

"We'll never give up! You hear me! I will never stop until I know the truth about you," the boss yells.

"You don't deserve her millions. That's what this is about. The mystery of millions. It's not fair!" the boss yells at the top of his lungs.

As Margaret and Alfred head down the hall. Everyone stops what they are doing and look at the boss.

"You need to calm down. Relax," Anna says. "Relax. I thought you were relaxed before they came in. What gives?" she asks, calmly.

He is still fuming, and his face is still red. Getting off the chair he heads into the workplace and looks at everyone. They quickly get back to work. He heads back to his office still fuming as he slams the door.

"It will never be over for me! Never!"

Anna looks at him calmly. It has been a while since she has seen him like this. He is a big man and overweight. As she sees him sweating she heads to the

fridge to give him a bottle of cold water. He drinks it

hurriedly.

"Maybe you should take ten. You know?

You're very upset. You're sweating profusely. This is

not good for you," she says, calmly.

Shockingly, he yells at her at the top of his lungs.

"Get out! Tramp!" he yells, as he points his

finger at her.

She hurries out of his office and closes the door.

Trying her best not to show everyone that she is upset,

she holds her head down for a moment and takes a deep

breath. Betty wants to say something to Anna. But she

decides to let her be. All of this will eventually calm

down. Anna gets off the chair and gets her purse. She

tells Betty that she will be back. Betty says that she

understands. As Anna leaves, the lady heads to the boss'

office. She knocks softly on the door and enters. He is

slumped on his desk.

"Are you alright?" she asks, softly.

"I will be okay. Close the damn door. No one

needs to see me like this. Close the damn door," he says.

She sits on the chair and does not say a word. He

knows what she is thinking. Gathering himself, he takes

a deep breath and heads to his private bathroom. He gets

a washcloth and puts cold water on his face. Turning off

the light he heads back to his office.

"Sometimes, as you know, some things you need

to let go. You need to just let it go," she says, softly and

calmly. "We're older, Ben. There are no guarantees in

life how long we will be here. We could have been gone

last night. This morning. Later today. With you being a

big man and your weight, you need to keep everything in check. I know how you feel. And I understand. But there's nothing that sticks out about him. Nothing," she says, handing him a manila envelope. "I did what you told me. I did the best that I could watching him. I'm not young like I used to be. You have little sweet Anna to do the groundwork and go over there as she did. I guess it did not work out with her. Did it?"

"No. She's a dime a dozen. You know what I mean? She's a good kid," he says, as his voice sounds kind for once. "But she is a go-getter, and she wants to succeed at a high level. You know how it is."

He looks at her face. She still has a sweet honest face. But now it is older with many wrinkles. Her teeth are yellow from drinking coffee over the years. And she was never one who liked going to the dentist. She was married once but that did not last long. She never had kids and when she would go on vacation, she would go with a group. That was how she had fun. She lives in a modest house which is a good size for her. She enjoys reading and collecting books. Lots of books. And she likes clocks. Anything that makes noise from a clock she must get one. When she comes home she always cooks. After dinner she usually falls asleep momentarily before she catches herself. Then, she washes the dishes and has dessert. Many people think that she lives a sad quiet existence life, but she was never one to complain.

"You've always been a good soldier. I'm sorry about how I get sometimes. I guess you think that I am one sad man. Huh? Or should I say you think that I am a sad rich man."

"I'm sure that you know the answer to that. Let it go. Please. Let it go. My God, man! You've got millions and will always have millions. You are a good smart businessman. Your ex-wife is happy thanks to your money. I know that you miss your daughter. But she is fine. Let it go. Please. For someone with money, if you die and there are no heirs, the worse thing is to let the government get it. Thank goodness you have a daughter. Claire knew what she was doing. That's why she went to that bar that night. She was not stupid. And when he came into the office I saw what she saw. He's a good man with a kind face. I have never seen anyone with a glow on their face like him. Interesting," she says, smiling.

"You're right. We've been acting stupid trying to find out about this stranger. Silly. Thanks."

She leaves his office. He reaches for his phone and dials a telephone number.

"It's me---Chief. I've come to my senses. Let it be. And let everything go. Everyone is right. I've been acting silly trying to find out information about him. Thanks. I'll give you a check soon," he says, hanging up the phone.

Meanwhile…

Margaret and Alfred are relaxing with a drink and chatting at her mansion.

She makes them another drink. He sips it because he knows that he will get a buzz.

He smiles kindly in return as he sits on the couch. She carries the drinks, and they sit together on the couch.

"That's where the office is. Huh?"

"Yes. That's it. Quite the zoo. Huh?" she asks.

"Yeah. I thought that it would have been nicer looking than it was. What a zoo."

"Yeah. He's quite the cheap miser. But he does give good bonuses. Of course, no one gets a good bonus other than little Anna," she says.

"I just don't get her. Is her life that sad that she-- is with him and---you know, does what he wants? People in the office know what's going on with them. Right?" he asks.

"Of course. That poor girl. As you said she has no scruples, and she has no class. I know that she is young. But I'm like you. I didn't sleep with just any man when I was younger. I had class," she says, with pride and dignity.

"I hear you. When you're sleeping with someone, you trust that person you're with. And you're also naked. You're exposed. Some people are okay with that. But not me. I was never one to just sleep with anyone for casual sex. I wanted a serious relationship with the person first and foremost before I had sex with them. I know that prostitution is the oldest profession in the book. But we know how dangerous it is especially today with diseases and so many prostitutes being murdered. I'm not saying that she is a prostitute. But when you have casual sex with people you're asking for trouble. The world is different today as opposed to when we were young. When we did it back then we did not think anything of it. And I don't know about you, but I did not sleep with strangers. I slept with someone from school who I knew."

"Yeah. I hear you. But there were a few people who I slept with that I did not know at first. They were okay. They came too fast. I know. Too much information. Sorry about that," she says, apologizing.

"It's okay. Nothing to worry about," he says.

The doorbell is rung, and they look at one another with shock on their faces. They're in disbelief that someone is ringing the doorbell.

"Are you expecting someone?" he wonders.

She shakes her head.

She gets off the couch and slips a bit. She laughs. Looking out of the curtains she hesitates. She cannot believe who it is as she opens the door.

"You? What are you doing here?" she asks, shocked and stunned.

"I would like to talk to him if that is okay," Betty says politely in her soft voice.

"You're not trying to mess up anything here are you?"

"Don't be silly. I would like to talk to him alone in his house. I just want to say some things to him. That's all. Please," Betty says.

Margaret opens the door. Betty enters and smiles when she sees Mr. Alfred.

"Sorry to bother you two. I would like to talk to you alone at your house. Please. I want to say something. Nothing else," she says, embarrassed.

"Don't be silly," he says, sipping his drink and frowning. "I'll uh see you later," he says, to Margaret, as he kisses her on the cheek. She blushes.

She closes the door as Betty and Alfred head across the street to his house. He unlocks the door, and

they walk inside. Closing the door, a gust of wind blew
it shut loudly. Betty jumps.

"Sorry. It was the wind. May I take your coat?"

"No!" she yells. "No. I will be fine. I just want
to apologize for all this. Listen. It's like this. Okay.
Everyone has been checking you out. Everyone wanted
to see who you are and who you were. Everyone. Yes.
Even her. Margaret. She likes you. She does. When
you kissed her on the cheek, I don't know if you saw her
reaction. But she blushed. I'm sorry the boss is an ogre.
He has always been that way. A rich unhappy ogre. As
for our little Anna. Little sweet Anna. Poor Anna. She
is smart and highly educated. But she---you know.
Fools around with him. We've done things in the past
when we were younger too but nothing like that. And
we did not make fools of ourselves a lot as she does.

But this is what she wants. And it makes her happy. So be it. So be it. Some of the things that they told you are not true. I am sure that they told you about the basement and they wondered if you looked inside there. There is no basement. Just a lot of rooms. She was---at one time, Claire, she delved into the occult. But it was nothing serious. Have you---have you witnessed her spirit?" she asks, as she takes a breath and stops talking.

"Oh. You know about that? Yes. I have. She is always with me late at night. She told me to be careful of everyone. I'm sorry that you're not happy. Your face is sad and unhappy. I'm sorry whatever happened in your life. But you will be okay. You're a survivor. May the Lord bless you, keep you and watch over you," he says, touching her face.

She smiles and blushes. Then, she opens her coat and exposes her sweater that reveal her big breasts.

"I've always been embarrassed by these two. That's all that men want to do is---touch them. Look at them. And suck on them. That has always bothered me," she says, softly, as if she is about to ball her eyes out any minute.

"No need to be embarrassed or to let that bother you. These days women get butt implants because they know that men like looking at women with big butts. Poor little thing," he says, as he tries to calm her.

"I used to have a nice figure for a bit a long time ago. But I am one of those women who eat and gained weight. Since there have not been a man in my life for some time---I just let myself go. Silly, I know."

He gets close to her and hugs her.

"As my brother told me years ago, be you. You are who you are. Oh uh---can we go into another room? I hate to tell you this, but Miss Margaret uses binoculars to look over here. I know. Pathetic."

As they go to the back room he hugs her and kisses her on her cheek.

"You can---you can touch them if you like. If not, I understand," she says.

"Please. Don't embarrass yourself like that," he says, shocked at what she just said to him.

"It's been a while since I have been with a man," she says, wiping her eyes.

"Have you seriously looked for a man?" he wonders.

"I have not. But---when you came into the office today, I said to myself I see why Claire fell for you.

You're a charmer and a good man. Believe me we can tell."

He looks at her sad hazel eyes and then he glances at her big breasts. She is a short woman about five-foot-four with short legs and hands. Her breasts stand out. He wants to touch them, but he stops himself. Momentarily, he leaves the room. He returns after a few minutes and hands her a manila envelope.

"What's this?" she asks, smiling. She opens the envelope and inside are 5 stacks of 10 one-hundred-dollar-bills. "I don't want your money. I'm fine."

"Use it however you want. As someone said to me years ago, if you have it give it. What's the use of having it if you don't share it. I'm sharing it with you. It's yours. Do whatever you want with it. Claire gave it to me. God gave it to her. Now I am sharing it with you."

She places the manila envelope onto the table. She takes off her sweater and shirt and then her bra. Her big breasts are exposed. He smiles and takes it all in. Hesitantly, and reluctantly he caresses them. She turns red.

"Wow. They feel good that's for sure. Wow," he says. He is about to lean over and lick them, but she moves back and puts on her bra, shirt, and sweater.

"I'm sorry. You must think that I am a pitiful old woman. Silly me," she says.

"I do not," he says, kissing her on the mouth. "You are not a pitiful old woman. I've been there with loneliness and no one in my life. It's a dark place and

lonely. It sucks. I understand. Did you want to talk
about it?" he says.

   "What is there to talk about? I've always been
the chubby girl who was smart. I don't have a nice ass.
My legs are short. All I have are my breasts and my
mind. When I was in school, my name was always
called first to get the test results. Then the kids in my
classes were nice to me. Sure, there were a couple of
guys when I was younger. We were young. They did
not last long, and they complained about how
uncomfortable they were being with me due to my
weight. They kissed me but they wanted to look at my--
-tits and play with them and lick them. Men," she says,
in frustration. "Oh, no offense to you. You're a sweet
guy. You do know that it's on your face? Your sweet,
kind face. Right?" she asks, looking at him in his eyes.

"I hope so. My mom always told me that. But I thought that she was being kind because she was my mom. I would like to think that I am a sweet, kind man. Thank you for saying that. I've been there with the loneliness. I know how you feel. It took me forever to have a serious girlfriend. My first wife was the one. The Lord had everything planned out for me. But at the time I did not know that. I figured it out once I divorced her. I was married after that. Big mistake. The choices that we make sometimes are the wrong choices. But through it all we must stand up and dust ourselves off. Have a good cry and be strong as we move forward. That is the key. When you don't do that, then you lose hope, and you end up harming yourself. No matter how tough things get, never give up. Move forward. Stand tall. Keep going. I know that I sound cliché but that's how I truly feel," he says, smiling.

She holds her head down and giggles nervously.

"Did you---did you like how they felt?"

"Huh? Oh, uh yes. I did. Yes. They look fine and they felt fine," he says.

"Even though they've sagged and hang down?" she asks, embarrassed, as her face is sad.

"You are older, correct? It's part of life, dear. Since we're on that subject---there was a time when I had issues keeping it up. I thought maybe because of the medication that I was taking for my arthritis and pain in my shoulder. But that wasn't it. It was because of who I was with at the time. I still like sex a lot. And I can keep it up okay. Of course, not as much as I did when I was younger. The weird thing is I am always hard in the morning when I must go to the restroom. Interesting. I know," he says, trying to keep a straight face.

She gets close to him. He can smell her sweet perfume. She holds her head up and looks at his face.

"Can I touch you? Do you mind?"

"Go ahead," he says.

Hesitantly, she touches his face, then she kisses him on his cheek. She touches him on his hips then she touches him on his leg and stops abruptly.

"I'm silly. I know. Sorry," she says, embarrassed.

"How long---uh---how long has it been since a man has been in your life?"

"If I told you, you would not believe me. Over ten years. I was never one for casual sex. Sometimes I want to have sex. But I am not that type of girl. I can't just have sex with someone because I'm horny. I only

have sex with someone who I am seeing. And someone

who I can trust and know that he is not seeing someone

else. You know what I mean?"

"Yes. I know what you mean. As I said we all

have made mistakes. And everyone has been lonely at

some point in their lives. I tend to give my heart away

too easily. This is why I have not been involved with

anyone in sometime," he says.

"Yeah but---but you know. You're sleeping with

her now. Right?" she presses.

"Yes. I know. We're older adults and we've

learned a lot from the past. I know that she is like the

others and have researched my background. I

understand that. But she seems as if she is okay. I had

to get used to the cosmetic work that she had done. But

I guess when you have the money, you can do whatever you please. I'm sorry that I never met you before. But hopefully, maybe, we can keep in touch. I would like that if that were okay with you."

"I would like that very much," she says. "Listen. I've held you up too long. And I'm sure that she is wondering what we're talking about."

"Screw her," he says, angrily as he frowns. "That's none of her business. If that is what is bothering her then she needs to get a life. I never wondered who she was talking to about me. You be careful. Okay?" he says.

"I know how to be careful. I'll try to get the ogre to leave matters be and let it go. Once he gets onto doing something he will never let it go until he sees it finished to the end. It is one of his many obsessions."

"Has he always been that way? How do you put up with it?"

"It's a job. I do my job well. I like the newspaper business. That's what I do. I work hard and do my best. I try not to get involved with other personal matters as our little Anna. She's young but she knows what she is doing. What a shame she is not interested in anyone her age. Sad. But she is an adult, and she knows what she is doing. She'll learn. Not everyone is meant to be in power or to be a professional and have an office with the view. She will grow up. Someday. Poor little thing. Let me go my friend. Thank you for listening and for not judging me for---that. Okay?" she asks, smiling.

"Of course, my dear. You sure you don't want any money? I have more than enough. When I have it I share it. I would like to share it with you. It's up to you.

Do whatever you want with it. Buy some new clothes or something or whatever. It's up to you."

"I'll think about it," she says, opining about the offer.

She reaches into her purse and pulls out a card, her business card with her cell number. She hands it to him.

"Call me sometimes. Whenever you want. When you're not with her. It's all over now. The searching about you on the net. Having the police search about you. But you know that---pig!" she yells. "Oh, I feel so much better saying that," she says, sighing and breathing a sigh of relief. "That ogre will not give up. He never does," she says, walking out of the room towards the door.

"You're very sweet and kind. Let me walk you to your car."

"It's right there on the street. I'll be fine," she says, looking at his eyes and face. "You're a kind soul with a sweet and kind face. Thank you. Oh. One other thing. Don't listen to anything that others have said about the basement. You probably have not explored this massive mansion. But there is no basement. Just a lot of doors. A lot of doors."

He watches her as she gets inside of her car, lock the doors, and drive off. He closes his front door and locks it securely. After turning off the lights downstairs, he heads to the bedroom. He takes off his clothes and puts on his nightshirt. Turning off the lamp he lies in the bed and stares into space. Soon, he falls asleep. Everything becomes quiet. Cold air fills the room. The wind rattles his window. Claire's spirit appears and leans over him.

"Safe now. You are safe now. Finally, it is over...but not for that evil man. He will never let it go because he is evil and unhappy. Let him keep researching about your life. There is nothing for him to see. He will find nothing about you because there is nothing other than what he knows about you. Relax now."

Margaret watches his house through her binoculars for a bit until she gets sleepy. Heading to her bedroom she gets into the bed when her phone rings. She hesitates to answer it.

"Yes?" she says into the phone.

"I'll never give in. Ever. You may have him now but for how long? You two have two things in common. You're both old and have money. I have youth and I know that I am hot. I can get any man that I want. You just watch your step. Just watch your step," Anna says, angrily, as she hangs up the phone.

Margaret runs downstairs and looks out of her curtains. She sees Anna in her car watching Alfred's house with her binoculars. After about an hour Anna drives off. She is tired and her eyes are heavy. As she is driving she slams on the brakes and barely misses slamming into a tree. She notices something in her backseat. Slowly, she turns around.

"What the---," she says, with fright on her face. "No way. No damn way."

"Yes. I am a spirit. We all have souls. I saved your life. You almost slammed into that tree. You need to grow up and let it be. If you do not let it be you will go mad! I don't think that you want to go mad. Do

you?" Claire asks.

"I don't believe this. No. Uh. Uh. There is no

way that I am in my car talking to you. A spirit. You're

dead. I believe in spirits but not this. No way," she

says, still in denial.

"You're right. You don't believe this and there

is no way that this can be happening. You're right.

You're right. You're right," Claire says, as everything

becomes black.

Moments later there are sounds of beeping. The

beeps become steady and louder.

"She's coming to, doctor. She's coming to," the

nurse says.

"I see," the doctor says, leaning over the bed

looking at Anna. "Can you hear me, Anna?"

"Huh? What? Yes. I can hear you," she mumbles.

"What were you trying to do? You are lucky to be alive. You barely missed a tree. Someone saw you slam on your brakes, and they checked on you. They called 911. What happened?" the doctor asks.

Anna looks around the room nervously at the nurse and the doctor. They are looking at her curiously and observing her.

"I think that she is still in shock, doctor," the nurse says.

"Yes. I agree, nurse. I will handle it from here, nurse."

"Yes, doctor," the nurse says, as she leaves the room.

The doctor waits for the nurse to leave and close the door. He looks at Anna.

"Now then little Anna. Do you remember me?"

"Oh. Yes. I do. I do," she says, embarrassed.

"You need to stop getting into other peoples' business. You were out there in your car late at night. Some things will never change. And some people will never change. I had hoped that you would have done something with your life other than work for that boss of yours. Maybe, perhaps, in time you will grow up. What happened in your car?" he asks, looking at her eyes.

"I was not alone. That woman---Claire, her spirit was there. It scared the heck out of me.

"For your sake and your health, you need to let it be and let matters be. That is not a good sign for you because that means she is watching you now. Everyone in the city knows the story about that man. Claire did

what she wanted. The more that you press on this matter

and get into that man's business, it will eat you up. As

you saw tonight it almost killed you. Stop this obsession

of yours. Are you doing it for the boss' sake or yours?"

he continues as he presses the issue."

"He's with that old dame who lives across the

street. They're---sleeping with each other. I flirted with

him in his house, but he was not having it. That makes

no sense. I can't let this go. I won't," she says,

sounding like a brat.

"For your sake you better. You need to grow up.

Rest now," he says, as he gives her an injection to relax

her. As he heads to the door to leave he looks around

the room before he leaves.

Claire's spirit sits on the chair and stares at Anna as she sleeps. A window in the room opens and cold air seeps in.

End?

"You are my mighty rock, my fortress, my protector, the rock where I am safe, my shield, my powerful weapon, and my place of shelter." Psalm 18:2

Keep chasing your dreams! Never ever give up. If you fall, get up. Dust yourself off. Start over. Go after your dreams! Dreams do come true!

Don't let others discourage you from your dreams. They are jealous, negative, or envious. Pay no attention to them. Go after your dreams. You are never too old to go after your dreams. Keep chasing after your dreams! Dreams...do come true!

Shh. Read. Listen to the mystery.